BETWEEN THE RIVERS

BETWEEN THE RIVERS

A WANDERER NOVELLA

(Set between *The Wanderer Reborn* and *The Wanderer's Legacy*)

NATASHA WOODCRAFT

ALSO BY THE AUTHOR

The Wanderer Series:
The Wanderer Scorned
The Wanderer Reborn
The Wanderer's Legacy
The Wanderer's Sister

The Wanderer's Sister is a novelette exclusively for
subscribers to the author's newsletter.
You can subscribe at:
natashawoodcraft.com/subscribe

This novella is set between *The Wanderer Reborn* and
The Wanderer's Legacy. The Wanderer Series as a whole
is based on Genesis Chapter 4 in the Bible.

CHARACTERS

Clarifications

Abba means Father. It applies most often to Kayin in Chanoch's voice, but also to other fathers.

Ima means Mother. It applies most often to Awan in Chanoch's voice, but also to other mothers.

Elohim means God. **Yahweh** is commonly translated LORD, but is God's name. They refer to the same being, **Yahweh Elohim**.

Characters in order of appearance

Chanoch (cHa-nok)	*Eldest son of Kayin and Awan*
Awan (Ah-wan)	*Chanoch's mother, 3rd child of Adam*
Channah (cHan-nah)	*Sister of Awan, 7th child of Adam*
Yael (Yay-el)	*Daughter of Channah*
Shiphrah (Sheep-rah)	*Daughter of Set*
Yemima (Yey-mee-mah)	*Sister of Awan, 11th child of Adam*
Set (Sheyt)	*Brother of Awan, 8th child of Adam*
Enosh	*Son of Set, husband of Yemima*
Adam (Ah-dom)	*1st man (Awan's father)*
Chavah/Ima (cHa-vah)	*1st woman (Awan's mother)*
Jared	*Cousin of Chanoch*
Talia	*Cousin of Chanoch*

MAPS

Eden
Realm of Leviathan
Northern mountains
R. Euphrates
R. Tigris
Kayin's Hill country
Eastern Mountains
The Lake
Settlement
Marshland
THE EAST

Eastern mountains
Entwined trees
Hills
Caves
Tigris
Farming land
Forest
Huts
Cliffs
Washing point
THE SETTLEMENT

The Lord is my light and my salvation;
whom shall I fear?
The Lord is the stronghold of my life;
of whom shall I be afraid?

Psalm 27:1 (ESV)

LEAVING

Must we go?' Chanoch asked for the fourth time, as he looked back at the meadow holding a hundred happy memories.

It wasn't the only place he'd lived. All over the land of Nod he'd wandered with his parents, and there were at least ten caves he might be tempted to call home. None of them were the place they journeyed to now. Once they crossed the mountains, it was unknown land. It might be vaguely familiar to his mother, who walked by his side, but even then, it was over half a century since she'd been there, and Chanoch never had.

'We must.'

Ima didn't elaborate further, for there was no point. Chanoch was sixty-five years old, and they'd put off this journey for long enough. Whilst they occasionally spied others in Nod, no-one there was a suitable candidate for marriage. The only people who ventured to their side of the mountains did so with evil intent. For their enemies had never ceased to hunt them and had come close to finding them several times. Only constant movement prevented it.

'What if we're met at the border?' Chanoch asked, aware that those very enemies dwelt in the territories they were heading towards.

'I've told you, my love, they do not seek us. It is only your father they are interested in.'

Chanoch found that hard to believe. He suspected that if Shimon's people ever did find them, they would leave none alive. Despite the tug in his heart that longed for a family of his own, on balance, Chanoch thought it was better to stay put than risk crossing the western mountains. Much could happen in half a century, and who knows what they would find on the other side? For all Ima knew, many could have left the land between the rivers. Shimon's clan might be the only people there.

As they reached the river path that they would follow all the way to the Great Lake, Ima stopped and squeezed his hand. 'Yahweh will protect us. He would not ask us to do something that would result in our death.'

She began singing as she continued walking.

> *The Lord is my light and my salvation.*
> *Whom shall I fear?*
> *The Lord is the stronghold of my life.*
> *Of whom shall I be afraid?*
> *Though the mountains quake and the seas roar,*
> *Yet I will be confident.*

It was the song she always sang on journeys, which usually happened due to suspected danger. A sighting here, an unexplained death there. Yet, in all their years together, Chanoch had never seen his ima panic. 'I learnt to overcome fear many years ago – when I first crossed the mountains,' she always said. She'd crossed them to find his father, and without that journey, Chanoch wouldn't exist.

By nightfall they had reached the lake, and they settled into a copse of trees. Chanoch knew this was the last bit of shelter and water for several days. They would carry coconuts with them for the journey across the plain, to supplement water collected from the only fresh spring nearby, for they could not refill their water-skins from the lake.

Though he had slept outside many times in his life, that night felt different to Chanoch. It was the turning point in their journey, for there was no going back once they entered the arid plain. They must press forward using the distant mountains as their guide, or they would get lost in the near-desert and might never emerge from it alive. Even in late winter, the plain could kill them.

'What are you thinking?' he asked Ima, as she stared into the distance. He could just see the outline of her face – unchanged since he was a boy.

'I am excited about seeing my siblings again. Yet, when I left all those years ago, Shimon promised he would blacken my name. He said I would never be able to return.'

'He did? Why?' Was there something about his ima's past he didn't know?

'I had done something terrible. I deserved it. Yet, my parents assured me I would always be welcome. We even discussed this plan, well before you were born. Still, it is strange, you know? Not knowing what has happened, how many babies there have been, who might have moved away. I hope Chayim and Avigail are still there, and I would so much like to see Dorit, and perhaps reconcile…'

Her voice trailed off, and Chanoch could hear the suppressed longing there. Chayim was her favourite sibling, the one she'd shared life most closely with until leaving the land between the rivers. She missed him, even all these years later.

So many sacrifices Ima had made to be with Abba. Now, Chanoch was expected to do the same. To leave his parents, all his siblings, everything he knew, to join a family he had never met. Could any wife be worth that?

Despite Ima's assurances, Chanoch was unsure they'd even accept him. Who would welcome the son of a murderer? What if such traits passed down the generations? Chanoch had barely a violent bone in his body, being far more inclined to run away and hide than to fight back, but that didn't mean his offspring couldn't inherit the blood of Kayin.

'What are *you* thinking?' Ima asked, turning his question back on him.

'That it will be a miracle if any woman between the rivers wants to marry me. Even if she does, the greater miracle would be her abba's acceptance.'

Ima gave the slightest snort and shuffled closer. 'My brothers are good men. Chayim has many fond memories of your abba, and Set is the most seriously moral person I've ever met. Neither of them would judge you.'

'Seriously moral? That sounds just like someone who would judge.'

'He's not a joker like Chayim. He takes everything seriously. But when I say moral, I mean Set journeys closely with Yahweh. He's always had a strong sense of right and wrong, and morality is about reflecting the whole character of our Elohim.'

'What do you mean, Ima?'

'Yahweh Elohim is not just fiercely holy and just, He is also kind and gracious, compassionate and loving. Doing what is right is as much about the latter things as the former. There is no sense in abiding by principles if we do so without love in our hearts. And without compassion, faith is meaningless.'

'I see. So, I'd better fall in love with one of their daughters then?'

She hummed, then emitted a chuckle. 'I have no idea how many women there might be now. Just don't choose Dorit. Though she is very beautiful, I think that would be stepping a little too far.'

THE MOUNTAINS

It took them three days to cross the plains and reach the edge of the mountains. Water was so sparse, they barely spoke to conserve their energy. As the high peaks loomed ahead, full of natural wonders and unknown danger, Ima paused and breathed deeply through her nostrils.

'It's a steep climb to the forests at the top, but once there, it's wonderful. I can smell the fresher air already, blowing down from above.'

She was right; the wind carried the scent of trees and felt different to the stifling atmosphere of the plain. Ima placed her hand on a gnarly trunk. 'There is a stream here somewhere, but it looks very different from last time I was here. There are many more saplings and I must remember, the trees I knew before have grown. I'm not sure if we've arrived at exactly the same place…'

She began shuffling around, inspecting the flora and fauna, until she spotted something. 'Several animal tracks cross here. They might lead to it.'

Chanoch followed her steady, soft gait, adding his footprints to those of the animals, just visible through the bracken. Ima had the better eyes, but then, she'd been living this lifestyle for longer. Eventually they came upon a small brook, and Ima's smile spread wide as she hugged Chanoch's arm, then released him to cup the water. It was the best water he'd ever tasted, though he suspected that was chiefly because this was the thirstiest he'd ever been.

After satisfying their thirst and refilling their water-skins, they sat down on a mossy rock. 'Are you ready for the climb?'

Chanoch could hardly say no. Though his legs were young and used to wandering far, it was his heart that protested. He looked back at the plain. Were it not so uninviting, he'd be tempted to refuse. A branch snapped in the trees behind them. Chanoch spun, expecting to find a spear-tip at his shoulder.

Some kind of weasel stared at him, then continued its way through the bush.

Ima threaded her fingers through his. 'It'll be alright, my love. The larger predators are on the next mountain range, and the climb up this one is worth it.'

Larger predators? Of course, the tanninim. Oh, why couldn't my father have come? Chanoch would feel safer with his strong abba nearby. *No, that's foolish; we'd be in greater danger with him and his mark.*

They had made it over halfway up the mountain before night fell and they stopped to make camp, find food and absorb the breathtaking views. As Chanoch gazed east, the lake they'd come from was visible, glinting in the sunset with silhouettes of flocks and herds adding to the ambience. *Might this be the last time I see it?* Chanoch thought as he drank in the view of his home – the land of Nod – while Ima snuggled into a mossy crag. As the sun descended behind him, sending the lake into darkness, he finally gave in, sighed and lay down with her.

She was already asleep. The steady rhythm of her contented breathing should have helped him rest, but instead it added to the conviction that he wasn't fit for a life without his parents. His calves ached from the climb, and he stretched his toes back and forth, trying to minimise the chance of cramping in the night. *Yahweh, can't you provide another way?*

Then the earth seemed to still. The noise of Ima's breathing, crickets chirping and flies buzzing ceased. His mind filled with something else – someone else.

Do not fear, He said. **I am with you.**

He stopped in the moment until gradually, the chirruping of creatures breached Chanoch's ears once more. Ima sighed and turned over.

The presence was gone. Had he imagined it? Could something so fleeting really have been Yahweh? *Was it You? Are You here?*

He recalled a story Ima had told him once, about her first journey to Nod. 'Yahweh is in the mountains,' she'd said. 'They are a special place. It's almost like we're closer to his dwelling place, for the air is thinner up there and He is more tangible.' She'd spent weeks in this area, talking to Yahweh, preparing her heart for its encounter with his father – the man who'd killed her twin brother. That experience had provided the spiritual sustenance she'd needed to journey on, to forgive and to endure. No wonder she slept soundly up here.

Chanoch allowed his tense neck to relax and closed his eyes. *Please, help me in the same way.*

The following day they entered the thickness of the forest, an area lush with wildlife and seasonal fruit. The humidity ensured a year round supply for the mammals that inhabited these lands. They stashed their packs with nuts and pomegranates and boiled the winter berries, leaves and roots, taking their time meandering through the paths and occasionally off them. Mammals hollered around, and in the distance, Chanoch heard the screech of the tanninim, but they were nowhere near.

Not so the day after. That part of the journey took them to the water-hole in the mountains, a gathering place for creatures from both sides. Monkeys swung on one bank while flying tanninim dipped their spear-like beaks into the water, and colossal creatures dominated the other bank, vying for position. The water was beautiful, but today, they were prey, and they didn't venture to the hot springs until night fell and the gatherings dissipated.

His mother's instincts and their collected supplies carried them safely over the next mountain, dominated by pine forests as far as the eye could see. The path was another steep uphill climb, accompanied by the frequent crashing of falling trees. Large tanninim dwelt here, knocking the trees over as they walked, but they did not encounter any that noticed them.

'You must have been terrified travelling this route alone,' Chanoch said, when a creature with a tail the size of a cedar had passed close by, making the ground shake with its footfall.

'I wasn't alone,' she said, smiling.

'But Chayim had already left you.'

'True, but Yahweh hadn't.'

Chanoch wondered if she'd experienced Yahweh the same way he had several nights before, but wasn't sure quite how to explain it in order to ask the question. 'Tell me more about Yahweh's presence,' he asked instead.

She did so as they sat before a fire that evening, for it wasn't safe to talk while on the path – you had to be constantly listening. 'One night I saw one of Yahweh's warriors,' she said. 'He was sitting outside the thicket I lay in, which he'd enclosed with light. He held a sword, a huge one, like I imagine the cherubim holding at the entrance to the Garden. I knew then that I had nothing to fear.'

My experience was nothing like that, Chanoch thought. *Perhaps it wasn't Yahweh, after all.* So he failed to share it.

When they crossed a river the day after, stepping single file over a fallen tree trunk, Ima seemed more nervous, and Chanoch noticed a tannin sitting on a far-off bank, eyeing them up. But it didn't venture closer. 'A bear chased me here,' Ima said as their feet touched harder ground littered with acorns. 'This water runs into the Tigris further down. We're unlikely to see more tannin now, but dangerous mammals still lurk.'

They had ventured another day's walk when the first signs of human habitation appeared. Cut pathways, shelters made with branches and palm leaves, burnt out embers. 'These are hunters' shelters. Shimon's people?' Chanoch whispered.

His ima hummed, her eyes flitting; alert. At any moment, people who knew this mountain far better than they did might find them. 'Let's try to minimise our tracks,' she said, slipping off the leather straps that bound her feet and holding them between her fingers.

Captured

T his time, the spear tip was real. Chanoch knew it, for heavy breaths accompanied it, and a mutter of, 'Don't move.'

Could he open his eyes? Did that count as moving? Senses sharpened, he sniffed deeply, hoping to catch the scent of his ima. He couldn't. His fingers twitched. Were hers nearby?

'You *can* open your eyes.' The words came out in a groan, almost sarcastic. It was a woman's voice.

Chanoch's eyelids fluttered open, immediately alighting on the sharpened stone held to his jugular. He gulped down the saliva rising in his throat. When his gaze flickered up, blue eyes met his. Bright blue like a summer sky. The young woman was pale skinned with light hair. He'd not seen anything like her before.

Amusement tugged at his captor's lips. She eased her blade away slightly – it was a small one, hand held, not a spear at all – and drew her shoulders down. 'Who are you?'

In his surprise, he almost blurted out, *Chanoch, son of Kayin*, but stilled his tongue just in time. The woman was dressed in skins, and her hair, though the colour of sunlight, was matted and screwed into a ball held up by a bone. Taught biceps bulged beneath strips of fabric tied around her arms, holding more weapons than just the one she threatened him with. She was a hunter, and certainly not a safe recipient of his name.

He pursed his lips, which seemed to set her against him.

'Fine, I will take you to my mother. She will know what to do with you.' She abruptly shouted, 'Get up!' which set Chanoch scrambling to his feet in a daze.

Then she tilted her head towards a large bush which a slight path led to – no more than an animal track. He stumbled that way, pushed on by the blade now resting between his shoulder blades. Only when he reached the bush did he see the gap in its centre, previously hidden by overlapping branches.

'Go through,' she ordered, and he obeyed, lifting a hand in front of his face to avoid being whipped.

The narrow track continued on the other side and they followed it for some time until he felt the blade lower. He ventured a glance over his shoulder just as the young woman put two fingers to her lips and emitted three shrill whistles – short, short, long. In response, a sheep bleated, and before Chanoch could figure out what that meant, he was pushed through another bush. This one did whip his face, for he had no opportunity to prevent it.

They came out into a clearing, where a few sheep grazed before a hut made from mud and straw. A fire burned next to it and before that, two more women sat. One looked uncannily like the woman holding a weapon to his back, and the other one was... *Ima!*

The unknown woman stood. 'This must be your son.' A smile hovered on her lips, and Ima turned her head.

As Ima called Chanoch's name and beckoned, a low growl rumbled behind him. Was that an animal, or…?

'Does that mean I must release him?' his captor moaned.

'It does, Yael.'

'Ugh!' The knife previously held to his back flew across the clearing and sank into the ground, perilously close to one of the sheep.

'Yael. Temper!'

Yael stomped towards her knife – in stark contrast to her silent footsteps moments before – then retrieved her weapon and slipped it into the band around her right forearm. Then she slumped next to the fire, put her chin in her hands and humphed.

By this time, Ima had reached Chanoch and was leading him forwards. 'Dearest, I'm sorry for leaving you alone. I was captured myself while collecting berries.' She chuckled. 'Channah has skilful daughters.'

'Channah?' he said. This must be Ima's younger sister, the one married to Shimon! Shouldn't they be afraid?

'Come, come, do not fear,' Channah said, encouraging him forwards. 'Would you like some stew?'

Chanoch ventured a glance at the pot suspended over the fire. Red meat, vegetables and grains. His stomach grumbled, but what meat was it? He'd heard the stories about Shimon…

Ima caught his eye and nodded. It seemed that whatever it was, she'd decided to accept Channah's hospitality. Indeed, a bowl sat empty next to her. Was she scared too – too scared to refuse?

'Yahweh is shining on you and your son, Awan,' Channah continued as she served him some stew and passed a bowl to Yael, who scowled before accepting it. 'My boys are hunting in the north today, and Shimon—'

'Where is Shimon?' Ima asked. Chanoch heard the slight tremor in her voice.

'He is in Nod,' Channah said. 'At least, I assume so. He has been gone two weeks with my eldest son. You probably just missed them. You know they regularly visit?'

Ima nodded. 'We know. We have seen the signs.'

'Were he here… had any of them found you—'

'Will your daughters tell?' Ima interrupted.

Yael looked up. 'Wait. This is her!' She leapt to her feet. 'This is the woman we were told to never let escape. Ima, you don't mean to let her go?'

Channah glared at her daughter, leaving Chanoch wondering if she'd shown kindness a moment ago, or if he'd imagined it.

'She's the murderer's wife!' Yael continued. 'And that means you—' Yael turned on him, and suddenly her knife was out once again, at his throat.

'Yael. Enough.' Channah's command stilled her daughter's attack and Yael bit into her lip, so hard that Chanoch spied blood. When Channah insisted Yael sit, she resumed the same cross-legged position she'd previously held.

Chanoch released a breath he hadn't known he was holding. This young woman was dangerous, but at least her mother held control.

'Awan is my sister. No-one, not even your father, has a right to take her life in my presence.'

'But he said we must keep her to use as—' Yael slapped a hand over her mouth.

Chanoch's feet itched. To use as what? They should leave right now and get as far away for this place as possible, but neither he nor his mother were fighters, and despite no other men being present, they didn't stand a chance if Channah wouldn't let them. Even if Channah were sincere, he had no inclination to trust this family. Indeed, Yael was probably the best of them, for at least he knew where he stood when she was incapable of holding her tongue. The only sliver of hope in this entire scenario was that Yahweh's name had graced Channah's lips. Ima claimed her sister was faithful – could it still be true after all these years married to their enemy?

Silence reigned as those around the fire considered each other. Chanoch glanced at Yael again, chewing on the lip she'd bitten, not noticing, nor caring about, the blood. She was younger than him, but not as young as she'd seemed at first. Tendrils of her hair had escaped her bun and a few un-matted strands now cupped her chin. Why wasn't she married? Then he realised his mother had mentioned another daughter. Where was the one who'd captured Ima?

COUSINS

Chanoch's unvoiced question was answered by a second shrill whistle and the loud bleat of a greater number of sheep. Soon sheep pushed into the clearing, followed by another woman of marriageable age, of darker skin-tone than her mother and sister and taller stature.

'Ah, she returns. Chanoch, this is my other daughter, my eldest-son's wife.'

'I brought back the sheep as you requested,' the daughter said, entirely ignoring Chanoch's presence. Her mouth curled into something resembling a snarl and Chanoch thought, *She might have been born a cat.* While Yael produced something between fear and fascination, this woman just made him want to run.

'So, you found him then,' she growled at Yael. 'Took you long enough.'

'Yael's attention snapped from her lip to her brother's wife. 'You don't know how long it took. You haven't been here. I was quick.'

'Not as quick as me.'

'Girls!' Once again, Channah played peacemaker. Did anyone in this family like each other? 'We are going to have a nice time getting to know each other with no more of this arguing.'

'I should very much like to know you all,' Ima said. 'For when I last saw her, your mother had no family, so you are all a wonderful surprise to me.'

What Ima said was true. They had known Shimon had accomplices, of course, for multiple sets of footprints evidenced his journeys to Nod, but they hadn't known the accomplices were his children. Channah had been barren when Ima left the land between the rivers a few years before Chanoch's birth.

'So tell me about your husband,' Ima continued, addressing her question to the newcomer. It was just like Ima to ignore the fact this woman had held her at knife-point and treat her the same as everyone else. 'Whom did you belong to before you married into this family?'

Channah's daughter-in-law pulled her cat-face again and walked off to inspect the borders of the clearing for errant sheep.

'My eldest son is a little younger than your son and is the spitting image of Shimon. His wife there is Dorit's daughter.'

'Dorit? She married?'

'Yes, she married our brother, Nadav.'

Ima released a whistle. 'Dorit always moaned about how annoying the triplets were and wanted nothing to do with them!'

'Yes, but Nadav turned out rather handsome, at which point she had a sudden change of heart. They are good together, but they left several years ago.'

'Dorit left?'

'Yes, they moved west with Chayim and Avigail, beyond the Euphrates.'

'So Chayim and Avigail are gone too?' Ima's face fell and Chanoch's heart reached out to her. She had been so excited about seeing her brother again, and his loss would hit her hard. Not to mention her hope of reconciling with Avigail and Dorit on this trip. She'd been praying the entire journey for that opportunity. 'I can't believe Chayim would leave the land he's tended all his life.'

'Set is in charge now,' Channah said. 'He runs the farmlands with his sons. When it grew crowded, Chayim volunteered to move on.'

Ima sighed. 'Chayim always was a peacekeeper.'

A shout from the other side of the clearing made everyone sit up. 'Yael. Get over here.'

Yael's eyes flew to her sister's, then she jumped up and departed, not before throwing another glare at Chanoch.

'Your girls are friendly,' Ima said in jest, but Channah didn't laugh.

'They're of the same opinion as my husband. You must understand, Awan; my children have been raised to believe their life's purpose is to find and kill Kayin. A man you chose to marry. You are a traitor in their eyes, sister. Indeed, you should never have come here. If you return to your husband, it will either be Yahweh's miracle or the circumstance that precedes Kayin's death. Which, I cannot yet say.'

The statement produced a chill in Chanoch's bones, tempered only by his proximity to the fire. Yet his ima merely smiled, claimed it was fortunate she believed in miracles, and continued talking to her sister.

Channah's daughters soon returned with a fleece retrieved from a dead animal and began to process it. The older one still refused to engage, but Yael occasionally shot Chanoch a look more piercing than her blade. Eventually, unable to bear the mothers' chatter about children and sheep, Chanoch rose and joined Yael where she was pulling wool, removing impurities and twisting it into a useable fibre.

'May I help?' he asked.

Yael didn't reply, but glared at him and carried on.

Chanoch watched her technique carefully – they'd never owned sheep, so he'd never learnt – then he grabbed a hunk of wool and copied her.

'You'll ruin it,' Yael said. 'It takes practice. And if you ruin it, Abba will beat me.'

'He still does that? How old are you?'

'How old do you think I am?'

'Thirty-five, maybe.'

'Ha. You age me.'

'What then?'

Yael sniffed. 'I'm going back out hunting.'

'Why?' Chanoch asked, noticing the brace of pigeons hanging from a nearby tree and the carcass they'd retrieved which the other daughter was attending to.

'To get away from you,' Yael said.

Laughter welled up within him and spilled out. It was a beautiful poultice for his fear-induced wounds.

Yael pursed her lips, but they twitched, and as Chanoch continued to release his amusement, she snorted. 'I hate you.'

'How can you hate me? We only just met.'

'You are weak. Scared. Pathetic. Abba would hate you. What are you doing here anyway?'

'I've come to find a wife.'

Yael's blue eyes caught the sunlight. 'Is that why you asked how old I am?'

'No!' The thought of marrying Yael was laughable. 'I asked it because we're cousins, and I was being friendly.'

'Abba taught us to distrust people who are friendly.'

'Why would he do that? The way Ima speaks about him, he enjoyed family life until Havel…'

'Until your father killed his favourite brother. You admit it?'

'It's no secret.' Chanoch caught Yael's gaze and wondered if she could sense his laughter turning to sadness. Did she feel emotions the same way he did? She was all passion and anger. Could she also feel compassion and love?

'Your father deserves to die.'

Chanoch nodded. 'He doesn't deny that. Yet, no matter how hard Shimon hunts for him, he never succeeds. Which is a good thing. Yahweh made a promise of vengeance, and Yahweh Elohim does not break His promises.'

Yael spat on the floor. 'That Yahweh stuff is nonsense. Ima still believes it, but I don't know why. Why should Abba be punished for enacting justice? It is Yahweh who is unfair, if He even exists.'

'He does. Our parents have seen his miracles with their own eyes.'

'I choose to believe what I see with *my* own eyes. And I see you, coming here looking for a wife when no-one here will have you because of whose son you are.'

'I expect you're right. Yet, here I am. So we may as well make the most of it. Do you know any of your other cousins?'

'Not really. Most of them live between the rivers. When I was a child, I played with Set's children.' Yael stared into the distance and paused, as if transported to a memory. 'Until Abba decided we were moving further into the mountains, then I didn't see them much.'

'I'm sorry,' Chanoch said, wanting to reach towards her but not daring to.

'Why?' she asked, looking genuinely confused. 'It's not your problem, is it?'

'Well, I've only ever known my siblings, and I have a lot. I'm the eldest of eight, and I'm not sure Ima's finished yet. I know brothers and sisters aren't always the easiest people to get along with, so I've always longed to meet my cousins. Fortunately, I'm very close to my parents.'

'Even the murderer?' She laboured over the word and Chanoch suspected that had it contained the right sound, she might have hissed.

'To me, he is just Abba.' *Though I know it's the truth, I can't imagine Abba ever killing someone.* 'Have you never done anything you were ashamed of?'

Yael's almost white brows drew together as she answered, 'No.'

'Really? Perhaps you don't understand then.'

'I don't. And I have no desire to spend any more time with you.' Throwing down her wool, she grabbed an extra spear, as if she needed more weapons, and ran through the bush they had entered by.

What are you really running from, Yael?

THE RIVER

When the sun dipped below the mountain, Channah gave them a sheepskin to sleep on. 'You can stay here tonight, but I dare not allow you to stay longer. There's no telling when one of the men will return.'

'Thank you,' Ima replied. 'We appreciate your hospitality, especially when we know it may cost you.'

A flicker of something crossed Channah's face. Chanoch couldn't tell what – it was too dark – but it made him uncomfortable, and despite being comfier than the previous nights, he struggled to fall asleep.

The following morning, they prepared to leave.

'You're just going to let them go?' The daughter-in-law was shouting at Channah behind the hut.

'She is my sister, and she is not the murderer.'

'Shimon will kill you if you let her go. You know this.'

'I am willing to take that chance.'

'You're crazy.'

As Chanoch hauled his refilled water-skin onto his shoulders, the shouter stormed into view and gave him a look that sent a shiver down his spine.

As they walked away from Channah's camp and headed towards the river crossing, Ima sang her song again, *The Lord is my light and my salvation. Whom shall I fear?*

Chanoch joined in, needing the words to quieten the niggling feeling that they had not seen the last of Shimon's family. What would be the consequences of Channah's kindness – would her husband really kill her? How could someone so bent on violence think himself any different from Kayin?

'It's downhill from here. If we press on fast without stopping, we should make it to the entwined trees today,' Ima said. 'Wildcats frequent this area – stay alert.'

Chanoch almost wished Yael and her blade were still by his side, but he hadn't seen her that morning – hadn't said goodbye. He wasn't sure why that bothered him.

Fortunately, Ima's songs seemed to keep the predators at bay and they did reach the entwined trees just before nightfall.

A more peculiar river-crossing he'd never seen. The mighty oaks on two sides of the Tigris had huge branches that looked far older than a few hundred years and joined together, creating a bridge across the water.

'So these are the miracle trees,' Chanoch laughed.

Ima grinned. 'They've grown a bit again, but mostly width ways, and not as much as they did before my eyes when I was with Havel.'

The scent of a salad of herbs carried on the breeze and Ima inhaled deeply. 'I always loved the hill-country. It was my favourite spot between the rivers. Well, aside from my fig tree.'

'The one Abba planted for you?'

'Yes.' Warmth spread across Ima's face and a familiar longing for his father manifested there. He'd seen it many times, when Abba was away and his mother stood watching every evening, waiting for his return. They loved each other so much. Enough to traverse mountains, perils and battle all bitterness in a relentless pursuit of each other. Would he ever find a love like that?

'Come, Chanoch. We must cross.'

Ima went first, showing remarkable tenacity in the face of the rushing river below. Chanoch trembled as he followed. If either of them lost their hold on the trees, they'd soon be in the water. Halfway across, he closed his eyes, taking a moment to breathe deeply. *Though the mountains quake and the waters roar, Yet I will be confident.*

When he opened them, Ima was safely standing on the other side. 'Come on!' she called.

Forcing himself not to look down, he continued, blocking the sound of crashing water with his voice. *Yahweh is the stronghold of my life, Yahweh is my stronghold, Yahweh is life…*

Soon his feet touched the ground. He relaxed, sliding his back down the trunk and collapsing to a seated position.

'We'll rest the night here, as you clearly need it,' Ima laughed.

'I thought you used to be terrified of water? How can you be so relaxed?'

'I was. Your father had to train me out of it. I have faced far worse things than water in my life. *Yet I will be confident…*'

They found a grove of trees in which to nestle out of the wind and settled down for their last night before potentially meeting Set. Would his uncle accept him? The uncle who never met Kayin? Or would he feel as Shimon did? Despite Ima's assurances of Set's character, he found Yael's assessment of his situation more realistic. He was the son of a murderer. What man would let his daughter near him?

When the sunlight flickered over Chanoch's face the following morning, the first thing he noticed was singing – beautiful singing. Was it Ima? It didn't sound like Ima's voice.

He rolled over. Ima was beside him, fast asleep. Trying not to wake her, he sat up and peered through the leaves of the copse. A woman was collecting herbs on the hillside, singing as she bent slightly awkwardly to pluck a stem, then twirling around once it was in her fingers. Chanoch noticed a slight limp in her gait, but it didn't affect the smoothness of her voice, which echoed through the hills.

Blessed are those whose delight is in Yahweh,
They are like trees planted by water,
Where leaves do not wither and fruits do not fail,
Whatever they do shall prosper.

She had a fairly plain face, but something sparkled in her eyes as she sang, transforming her features. She was slightly plumper than Chanoch's sisters, though most of them took after his father with his enormous height, and his mother with her slight build. Chanoch supposed this woman was a similar height to him, or perhaps slightly shorter. For he'd never resembled his father.

'Shiphrah, hurry up! Must you always take so long?'

The call came from further down the hill, and Chanoch couldn't see the voice's owner, but Shiphrah looked up, laughed and shouted back.

'Why should we rush? It's a beautiful morning and it takes me so long to get up here, I may as well enjoy it.'

'Because Abba insists on me accompanying you, which is extremely tiresome when I have a horde of other things I would far rather be doing.'

'I don't know why he insists on it,' Shiphrah answered. 'It's not like we ever see anyone else on these hills. What could possibly happen?'

'Do you really need to ask that question?' A tall, lanky youth came into view, striding up the hill. 'At any moment, you could collapse, fit or worse. Plus, there are wild animals in these hills. If something ever happened to you on my watch, Abba would never forgive me.'

Shiphrah approached the young man and threw her arms around him, though she could only reach his chest. 'I love you too, brother. I'm glad you care so much for my welfare, and not just for your own.' She chuckled and tickled his side. 'Do you really have lots to get on with? Couldn't we have a few moments watching the pictures in the clouds? It's such a beautiful day.'

The lanky youth sighed and sat down. 'Fine. Just a few.'

Chanoch watched with interest as Shiphrah lowered herself using her brother's hand for support. It seemed her right leg didn't bend correctly, and her back was slightly misshaped. When she finally had her bottom on the floor, she lay back and stared into the sky. Chanoch could barely see her above the seed heads of the grass until she raised an arm.

'A wildcat – look!'

Her brother chuckled then pointed in a different direction. 'There's a two-legs, coming to eat your cat. It's moving, moving, ah! There it goes.'

Shiphrah laughed, and the sound rang in Chanoch's ears as sweet as her melodic voice had done before.

'That one looks like fire,' she said. 'How peculiar. Do you think it's Yahweh?'

'In the clouds? I doubt it.'

'He comes in the fire though, doesn't He? That's why we sacrifice.'

'But that, Shiphrah, is simply a cloud.'

'What about the wind, then? If He speaks in the wind, surely a cloud isn't too far-fetched.'

'Your imagination is always far-fetched. I've never seen Yahweh, nor heard Him. What would I know?'

'I hear Him,' Shiphrah said. Her voice was quieter and Chanoch had to strain his ears to catch her words.

'Yeah, right. Who are you, the next Havel?'

'No, I'm not claiming that. But I'm quite sure Yahweh speaks. Often I simply must do something, and receive no peace until I do it.'

'What, like lie on the grass and stare at the clouds? I received no peace until you got to do that.'

'Oh, shush. I won't talk with you about it if you can't be serious.'

'Wonderful. That's all I was hoping for.' The young man jumped up and held out a hand. 'Come on. Aunty will be wondering where you've got to.'

Shiphrah sat up and smirked. 'She won't. She knows I'd spend all day here if I didn't have such an impatient guardian.'

Shiphrah's brother helped her up and then held her arm as they walked back down the hill. However much he teased, it was obvious he cared for her very much.

'They seem rather lovely.'

Chanoch jumped at his ima's voice. 'How long have you been awake?'

'Oh, quite a while. Why didn't you introduce yourself?'

'I expect for the same reason you didn't. It felt like we were spying. What was I meant to do, crawl out of the bush and frighten the life out of them?'

Ima chuckled. 'I suppose not. Are you hungry, or can you wait until we reach their home? They can't live far away if that young lady made it up here by first light.'

Chanoch's stomach grumbled, but the thought that he might soon have a decent breakfast, and get to meet Shiphrah properly, was enough to convince him to press ahead. 'I can wait.'

They found Shiphrah's home easily, for her brother wasn't expecting to have trackers and failed to notice them following behind.

'It's a good thing we're not predators,' Chanoch murmured as they approached. 'He's not the most effective guardian, is he?'

'He hasn't lived a fugitive's life like you have,' Ima replied. 'When I was young, I spent time alone on these hills often.'

'Weren't there predators?'

'Not many. I was more nervous after your abba was attacked by wolves, but they tended to hunt at night and I only ventured out during the day.'

They'd been spotted. Not by Shiphrah or her brother, but by another woman standing by the fire.

'Is that—' Ima quickened her pace.

The woman straightened her back and jolted forwards. 'Can it be… Is it possible?' she called.

Chanoch couldn't guess who this was, but the two women clearly recognised each other. The former broke into a run, coming towards them with arms wide, and Ima vaulted into her embrace.

Before Chanoch had reached them, he heard the cries of joy. 'Awan, I can't believe it's you! How long has it been? Abba. Abba, come quickly.'

A man emerged from the hut. He was of average build and height and had shoulder length, dark-brown hair and a beard that covered his neck. He looked older than anyone Chanoch had seen before, but not by much.

Ima burst into tears as the man grasped her shoulders, kissed her, then drew her into a tight embrace. 'My darling girl, my darling girl,' he kept repeating.

Could this be her father? Could it be…

Ima pulled herself free, turned and beckoned towards him. 'Chanoch, come.'

As he drew nearer, he saw the semblance between the features of Ima and the woman she'd hugged. 'This is my sister, Yemima,' Ima said, 'and this…' Ima squeezed the man's hand, 'This is your grandfather.'

So it was Adam, the first human. The man created by Yahweh himself. Adam smiled and spread wide his free arm. 'Come, my boy. Welcome. You are very welcome here.'

Family

The words sent warmth flooding through Chanoch's body. Could it really be true? He was welcome? The son of Kayin? It was all very well for his ima; she had grown up with these people, had loved them for half her lifetime but he... he didn't even know them.

'Come, sit; we must get to know one another. I was just about to leave to check on the sheep, but they can wait today,' Adam said.

'I'll go, Sav.' The lanky youth reappeared, studied Chanoch with curiosity, then grabbed a leather pouch hanging nearby, and a sling.

Ima sat beside his grandfather, still holding his hand, and leaned against his shoulder. As she sighed and closed her eyes, Chanoch witnessed a peace descend on her face; a satisfied longing. He'd known she'd missed her family, but only now did he realise how much she'd sacrificed to stay in Nod.

Yemima introduced the various young children running around, then sat on Ima's other side and snuggled into her, receiving an arm around her shoulders in return. 'You must sing to us,' Yemima said. 'No-one can sing as you do, and I've missed you so much. It took me a long time to forgive you for abandoning our morning cuddles, and not until I married did I experience such joy again.'

'I'm sorry,' Ima said, 'I missed them too. So much. I thought you might have changed beyond recognition and was so thrilled to recognise you instantly. But there's one thing you are wrong about.'

'There is?'

'Your daughter, Shiphrah, has a wonderful voice.'

'Oh,' Yemima chuckled. 'Shiphrah isn't my daughter.'

'She isn't?'

'I married Set's second son, Enosh, whom of course you haven't met. Shiphrah is Enosh's younger sister, Set's third daughter.'

'Everything has changed so much! It will take me an age to work out all the new family connections.'

'How do you know about Shiphrah's voice? Have you met?' Yemima asked.

At that moment, Shiphrah emerged from Yemima's hut, blushed and went to sit the other side of Adam. Chanoch tried to watch her subtly, desperate to study the contours of her face up close, but not wanting to look like he was staring.

'We heard her singing on the hill. It's how we knew there was a home nearby,' Ima replied. 'We held back so we wouldn't scare her by emerging from the undergrowth.' Ima reached towards Shiphrah. 'Apologies, my dear.'

Shiphrah whispered something in Adam's ear. She hadn't seemed shy on the hill, but now in the company of strangers, she was. Chanoch could relate. He preferred quiet moments and, never having met people who weren't his siblings or parents before, he was struggling to know what to say himself. Strange how he hadn't had such difficulties with Yael.

'My granddaughter was asking me who you are,' Adam said. 'Shiphrah, this is Awan, my daughter who lives with Kayin in the east, and her son, Chanoch.'

Shiphrah nodded, cupped her hand and whispered something else.

Adam turned to Chanoch. 'This is rather forthright, but, she wants to know why you are here.'

Ima chuckled and saved Chanoch from answering. Though he'd happily confessed their intentions to Yael, he now felt embarrassed to reveal them. 'There are no other persons in Nod,' Ima said. 'Chanoch only knows his siblings. It was always our intention to bring him back here when he was old enough to marry, but I've taken a long time to do it. Mostly because I can't bear the thought of parting from him.'

She'd explained it more delicately than he would have, but still, Chanoch stared at the ground, not willing to risk catching Shiphrah's eye.

Incredibly, Ima's words seemed to loosen Shiphrah's tongue. 'You've never met anyone other than your siblings?' she asked him.

He had to look up then. It would be rude not to. Peeling his eyes from the grass, they found hers and he was momentarily lost. Up close, they were almond-shaped, but chestnut in colour. She had long black eyelashes that reached her cheeks when she blinked, and suddenly, she didn't look plain at all. A beautiful, hidden soul shone through.

Chanoch stammered. 'N-n-no… No. Well, until a few days ago.'

When he didn't elaborate, Ima did so. 'We met Channah and her daughters in the mountains.'

Chanoch noticed Adam stiffen. 'And she let you go?'

Ima nodded. 'Mercifully, Shimon and his sons were absent.'

'That was Yahweh's timing, for sure. If Shimon finds out…' Adam's lips trembled as if a shiver had run through him. 'We have not had much to do with them for a long time.'

'I gathered that, and I am sad for it. I should have dearly liked to have seen them all.'

'No, Awan. You must never meet Shimon again. Do not wish for it. When you return to Nod, you must do so by a different route.'

Adam's grave tone produced silence for a few moments before Yemima broke it. 'You can't have eaten yet. Let me get you something.'

She hopped up and disappeared into her hut, emerging moments later with fruit and bread, which Chanoch hungrily devoured. He noticed that Shiphrah didn't eat anything. She must have had breakfast already, but walks on the hills usually gave him an appetite for seconds.

'Where's Ima?' his mother asked, and it took him a moment to realise she meant her own mother; he was so used to *Ima* referring only to her.

'She's at home, in the same hut you grew up in,' Adam said. 'I often spend nights up here in the colder months, for the grazing is better here. And Enosh often stays with Set, for he farms in the valley. Set has expanded the farmlands considerably since you left. You'll barely recognise it now.'

'I heard that Chayim moved away,' Ima said wistfully.

'Yes.' Adam stroked her hand. 'I am sorry you won't meet them again. But Yahweh commanded us to fill the earth, and we must spread out as we multiply.'

'I wonder how big the earth is?' Shiphrah murmured to herself, but Chanoch heard. She was staring out towards the hills they'd come from.

'And you, dear,' Ima asked her. 'Do you live here or in the valley?' She must have missed Shiphrah's mumble.

The younger woman looked at Adam again, willing him to answer for her. She tilted her chin, but he merely chuckled and said, 'Don't be shy, girl. They are family.'

'Everyone is family, Sav,' she said, which made him chuckle again, before giving in.

'Shiphrah is not able to farm the larger crops or to be a shepherd. She accompanies her younger brother here, whom you met earlier. He helps me with the sheep, while she helps Yemima with the children. With Enosh often away, the arrangement works well. Awan, I was thinking I would return to your mother tomorrow. I miss her. You can stay here the night and then come with us, if you like?'

'I would like that immensely. If I could run to Ima now, I would, but spending time with Yemima is wonderful also.'

'Perhaps in the valley, we can introduce your son to some young women, hey?' Adam winked at Chanoch. 'Raham's girls are particularly lovely.'

The thought of being introduced to more people already did not fill Chanoch with joy. He wanted to stay here a while and spend time with the ones already present. But he wouldn't deprive Ima of seeing her mother. And he had to admit he was curious himself. The woman who took the forbidden fruit… What would she be like?

THE SONG

They spent the rest of the morning catching up on family news. With no frame of reference, Chanoch found it hard to keep up with all the names and connections, and he soon switched off and watched Shiphrah playing with the children and doing chores. When he tried to get up to help, Yemima insisted he stay seated after his long journey, and brought him more food.

Ima sang several of the old songs and Yemima joined in. Some of them he noticed that Shiphrah knew too, for her voice reached him even though she sang as quietly as possible.

When Adam got up and said he must relieve Shiphrah's brother, Chanoch took the opportunity to rise also. 'Do you have any wood I could chop,' he asked Yemima, 'or grain to grind?'

Yemima laughed and pointed him towards a large, flat stone. 'If you insist. There's a sackful in the store.'

Ima soon spied Yemima's laundry basket and the sisters decided to wander to the brook together. 'You'll be alright here, Chanoch?' Ima asked, and he happily agreed.

From his position at the grinding stone, Chanoch could see the small vegetable garden behind the hut, which Shiphrah was now attending, showing two of the children how to thin the seedlings – reserving the baby roots and leaves for salads, while allowing the others to grow larger. It was a similar technique to what his abba had taught him. Kayin could never cultivate crops, only harvest from the wild. It was Yahweh's curse upon him.

Now you are cursed from the ground, which has opened its mouth to receive your brother's blood from your hand. When you work the ground, it shall no longer yield to you its strength. You shall be a fugitive and a wanderer on the earth.

When Kayin had tried to work the ground in the past, the results had been disease and death of the plants. Yet his father retained the knowledge he had gleaned from the years before Havel's death, and this he had passed on to his children – instructing without touching.

'It is my curse, Chanoch,' Kayin had told him. 'There is no reason why you cannot one day settle with a wife and tend the ground. So I will teach you all you need to know.'

Chanoch longed to join Shiphrah now but didn't want to frighten her. She glanced at him every so often, a tentative smile touching her lips. Then he had an idea.

Blessed are those whose delight is in Yahweh,
They are like trees planted by water…

He didn't think much of his own singing voice, but when she recognised the words and tune, she gave him a longer glance. Then she joined in.

Where leaves do not wither and fruits do not fail,
Whatever they do shall prosper.

The song was really a duet, and the boundaries of mountains and time hadn't changed that. As their voices joined together in harmony, they both stood straight and they instinctively moved closer, their steps aligning.

Not so those who fail to trust Him,
They are chaff blown on the wind,
Reaching the sky.
Yahweh Elohim, grant that we may be,
Delighted in You, the Most High.

'You know it?' Shiphrah said, as the song ceased and their fingers touched.

'Ima taught me. Your abba composed it, I believe?'

Shiphrah nodded. 'My mother and father together. It was the first thing they sang as one.'

'I heard you singing it on the hillside earlier,' Chanoch confessed. 'I saw you with your brother.'

Emitting a sigh, Shiphrah studied the lines on her hands. 'Then you saw my foolishness.'

'No. What can you mean?'

'I am a dreamer. I stare into the sky and imagine...'

'I don't think it's foolish.'

She looked up. 'You don't?'

'You... you captivated me.'

With a snort of disdain, Shiphrah abruptly pulled her hands away and returned to the vegetables. 'Now I know you are playing with me.'

Chanoch shook the stupidity from his head. Why had he said that? He'd only just met her.

With a wince and a grunt of effort, she lowered herself to the ground, while he fought the urge to reach out and help. 'You see, I am an invalid,' she said.

'What does that matter?' he asked, coming to his senses and kneeling beside her. He may be terrible at communicating, but it pained him to see her demean herself.

'My mother was sick when she carried me. She'd eaten something off and it wracked her body for weeks. When I came out, I wasn't like everyone else. My back wasn't straight and I took years to learn to walk. When I was five, I started fitting. Falling over with no explanation or warning. When I was eight, I became seriously ill and almost died. The family held vigil for weeks, sacrificing and praying for my deliverance. Yahweh spared my life, but I was not healed entirely. I still have the same problems as before. I am now fifty, and not once has a man shown interest in me. Who would desire being burdened with this?'

'But you are happy.' It was a statement, for the image of her twirling on the hillside was burned into his mind.

Having gardened throughout her speech, keeping her gaze firmly on the ground, Shiphrah glanced upwards now. Her almond eyes met his, and his heart melted a little more.

'I am.' She smiled. 'Because I love the One who spared me, and I love those little terrors...' She motioned to the children who'd gotten bored with this peculiar conversation and begun running around chasing each other. 'I don't need anyone else.'

In other words, she didn't need him. 'What I said – about you captivating me. It just, sort of, found its own way out of my mouth. I'm not good at talking to people. I usually prefer my own company. I'm sorry if I made you uncomfortable.' He pulled a young root vegetable from the ground and rubbed it between his fingers, removing the mud.

Shiphrah nodded. 'That's alright. I suppose you have your own difficulties, not knowing anyone but your siblings. Is it lonely there, in Nod?'

Chanoch thought about it. 'I suppose those who are used to something different might find it lonely, but I find it peaceful. Of course, we live as nomads, always wandering, moving any time there's a sign that our tracks have been found or hunters might be close…'

'Hunters. You mean predators?'

'No. Well, sometimes. But mainly, we are on the alert for Shimon.'

'So he really does hunt Kayin?'

Chanoch nodded. 'For the most part though, we live in peace, surrounded by the beauty of Yahweh's creation, worshipping him as we walk and, occasionally, talk. I'm the quietest of my siblings. I spend more time with Abba than the rest of them. He's not a big talker either.' A yearning for his abba's presence hit him as he realised this was the longest they'd ever been apart.

'It must be terrifying. Coming here and meeting all these people you don't know.'

'Do you know what scares me most?' Chanoch said.

Shiphrah shook her head.

'The thought that I might fall in love with someone who will reject me.'

'Why would anyone reject you?'

'Because of who I am. You are a daughter of Set, Shiphrah. I… I am a son of Kayin.'

Understanding passed between them. They were not so different, for they both feared what they were.

THE VALLEY

The day was over too quickly and soon it was nighttime. Chanoch enjoyed the luxury of a sheepskin again as Shiphrah's brother sacrificed his bed for the guests.

The following morning, they prepared to leave with Adam. Chanoch was anxious to find Shiphrah before they left and managed to locate her at the brook, washing her face. 'Sorry, I didn't mean to disturb you. I just wanted to say goodbye.'

He helped her to stand and her hand remained in his. 'I'm sorry we didn't have more time.'

Shiphrah looked sadder than even he felt.

'What is it?' he asked.

'Nothing. Just… thank you for sharing your heart with me. As you are forced into the company of my more beautiful and accomplished relatives, I hope you won't forget I exist entirely.'

'Forget you, Shiphrah? It's not possible.'

Shiphrah turned away. 'I have no expectations, Chanoch.'

'What do you mean?' He shuffled around to face her again.

'I mean, I know you will find a wife there. My abba is a just man and he will not hold your father's sins against you. But when you leave with your wife, perhaps you will do so with happy memories of me?'

'Leave with my wife? No, you misunderstand. I am to stay here, in the land between the rivers.'

'You are? Why?'

'That has always been the plan. "A man shall leave his father and his mother and hold fast to his wife, and they shall become one flesh." Those are Yahweh's words. It is Nod and my family I must leave behind. You and I… we will see each other again.' *Besides, I do not expect to find any woman I like as much as you, but I dare not say that now, or I will scare you off again.*

Shiphrah's face brightened. 'Then I will see you again? I am glad. I was just beginning to like you. Though I feel sad for you…'

'Why?'

'Your heart longs to return to Nod,' she whispered softly.

He had never confessed it, but she had seen straight through him. He took her fingers and twiddled them between his own. Was he allowed to touch her this way? He had no idea. He'd never been close to a woman who wasn't his sister or mother before. Somehow though, it felt right. *She* felt right. 'I'm sure I will adjust to life here in time. Thank you for noticing.'

Before she could draw closer, he dropped her hand and began walking away. If he didn't leave, he might do something else that he was fairly sure *wasn't* appropriate. 'I'll see you soon.'

As they trundled to the valley, Adam led the way. It was slow, for the sheep wandered in front, with Shiphrah's brother on their flank, keeping them contained. Ima walked beside Adam, remarking on all the changes in the landscape since she'd last been here. After a while though, she noticed Chanoch dragging behind and came to join him.

'Are you alright, dearest?' she asked.

'Yes. I would have liked to have spent longer with Yemima; do you think we could visit them again?'

'Of course. Shiphrah is a lovely girl.'

'You thought so?' He shouldn't be surprised. Ima always judged people by their heart rather than their appearance.

'You like her, don't you?'

'I've only just met her.'

'Yet she seems to suit you. You are both gentle souls.'

Chanoch didn't feel comfortable having this conversation yet. What was he meant to say? These emotions were entirely new to him; he didn't really understand what they were. All he knew was that the memory of Shiphrah's voice had lulled him to sleep last night, and he could still feel the touch of her fingers on his palm.

Ima smiled and threaded her arm into his. 'There is no rush. We're here now. You can take as long as you need. You don't even need to decide before I leave.'

They hadn't yet discussed Ima's return, how long she intended to stay or whether it was safe for her to return on her own. Despite having crossed the mountains in the past, the thought of Ima undertaking the arduous journey alone filled Chanoch with dread.

It was mid-afternoon when they spied farm workers tilling a field. One of them, a stocky man of average height, with sandy, short hair, immediately called out. 'Abba. Is that you? Who's with you?'

Adam called back. 'A surprise.'

The man dropped his tool and began to jog forwards, while a second person, who looked similar but younger, held back and watched.

Ima burst into laughter. 'It is him. It is Set!' She tugged on Chanoch's arm and ran towards the jogger until she met her younger brother with a squeal.

'Awan? Awan! Praise Yahweh, what are you doing here?' As he lifted her and spun her around, Ima threw back her head and laughed towards the hills. Then she snuggled into the man's neck. They held each other for a few moments before breaking apart. Then Set clutched her face. 'Look at you. You haven't aged a day.' He laughed. 'But who is this?'

Set had turned and fixed his gaze on Chanoch. Chanoch noticed his uncle's eyes were the same as Shiphrah's, without being so feminine.

'This is my eldest son, Chanoch,' Ima said, then cupped her hand and whispered in Set's ear.

His eyes widened and he whistled. 'I see. Well, you'd better come meet the family, then. Boys, stop work. There are more important things to do today.' Set waved to the other workers and Chanoch saw there were actually six in this field. Some had been working in a ditch, hidden from immediate view.

Set slapped the nearest on the back. 'My son, Enosh. Enosh, this is your aunt, Awan, and her boy, Chanoch. I assume, as you're with Abba, that you've already seen Yemima? This is her husband.'

'Yes. It's wonderful to meet you, Enosh.' Ima kissed her nephew on the cheek, but aside from enquiring about her journey, Enosh said nothing. Chanoch thought he might be shy like Shiphrah, but as they departed, in what Chanoch presumed was the direction of Set's home, Enosh came to join him. 'Did you find my wife well?' he asked. 'I haven't been home this week.'

'Yes, she is well. And your children, and Shiphrah.'

Enosh nodded. 'Good, good. I hate leaving them. I worry about her being so near the mountains. But I must help here sometimes. There is so much to do to feed us all.'

'I understand. How many live here?'

'Between the rivers? Oh, around one hundred now, I think. No, it must be less, for my older brother left a few years ago with his family. That's when I started staying down here to help Abba. I tried to convince Yemima to move down too, but she loves it in the hills.'

'I don't blame her. You have a beautiful home.'

'So, you're looking for a wife?'

News travels fast.

'You should consider my sister, Sarai. She is next in line to wed and reasonable-looking.'

'Thank you…' Chanoch didn't know what else to say.

'There's also Raham's daughters – he has two unmarried. My younger brothers are vying for their attention, but you might get lucky.' Enosh continued to rattle off several names, but he mentioned nothing other than their looks and connections.

Are they kind and generous? Do they love Yahweh? These are the things Chanoch wanted to ask, but he didn't find the courage.

When they reached Set's home, Ima had more reunions to attend to. Set's wife cried and hugged her, then two of Ima's triplet-brothers appeared, who barely remembered her even though they were older than Yemima. Each had wives and children to introduce, which included Raham's daughters, who were as beautiful as Enosh had described.

After they'd been there a short while, an older woman came running from the west, followed by Adam. Chanoch hadn't even noticed Adam leave – there'd been so many coming and going. Long, black curly hair flew behind her, and she ran with ease, despite carrying a heavy basket. Throwing the basket down just before she reached them, she shouted Ima's name.

It was Chavah, Adam's wife. The first woman, his ima's mother and the forbidden-fruit picker. What would their lives have been like if she'd never succumbed to temptation? Would they be different? Or would someone, eventually, have believed the deceiver's hiss?

This reunion was the most emotional yet, surpassing all previous encounters, and Chanoch patiently waited for the tears to subside. Chavah didn't seem any different from anyone else, just as Adam hadn't, and it was clear that whatever she was like, Ima adored her.

'How long has it been?' Enosh asked. Chanoch had forgotten Yemima's husband was beside him.

'I am sixty-five, and she left a few years before I was born,' he replied.

'It's strange, isn't it? If she loves her family this much, you'd think she would have left The Wanderer ages ago, and come home.'

The Wanderer? What a strange thing to call Abba. Do you not realise you are speaking of my abba?

But Enosh didn't seem to, or at least couldn't see beyond his curse. *I'm glad your sister isn't like you,* Chanoch thought. *Shiphrah sees me.*

'So what did you make of Sarai? Alright, isn't she?' Enosh continued. Chanoch hadn't paid much attention, but now he forced himself to look at Enosh's other sister.

'We wouldn't mind if you took her back to Nod,' another man who'd been in the field with them said. Chanoch thought it was one of Set's younger sons, but he was lost in a sea of faces and names. 'Whereas if you take one of Raham's girls, we'll all miss the scenery.'

Chanoch's blood ran cold as the men chuckled. Did he imagine it, or had they just referred to the women as *scenery?*

He studied the speaker, trying to commit his features to memory. *If there is one friendly person I shouldn't trust, surely it is this one,* he thought, remembering Yael's words. As he did so, he became convinced this wasn't one of Set's sons. 'I'm sorry, I missed your name?'

'I'm Jared, son of Shalom.'

Shalom… Chanoch racked his brains. *Ah yes, the third triplet.* So, those girls were his cousins. Ah, everyone was a cousin. It was so confusing.

'Are you married, Jared?'

'No,' the man laughed. 'Still on the lookout, my friend. Any of your sisters available?'

Not to you. Chanoch shook his head. 'My parents would see me wed first, then they will consider the others.' He realised he should try to remember as many of these men as he could. For if any of them came to Nod, interested in his sisters, he wanted to have a grasp of their character to relay back to Abba. Then he recalled he wasn't going back to the land of wandering, and his heart sank once more. *I will likely not see my sisters again. In sixty years' time, will it be me journeying back and greeting my long-lost family as Ima does now?*

He made a mental note to inform Ima about Jared anyway, just in case.

SHABBAT

For the rest of that week they stayed in the valley, sleeping in Set's home with his numerous offspring – some adults, some children. During that time, Chanoch didn't set eyes on Shiphrah again, nor did he meet any other woman that commanded his attention. Though some were truly beautiful, their loveliness failed to capture his heart.

'It's not like they would want me anyway, even if I wasn't Kayin's son,' he said to himself as he walked by the river on Shabbat morning. 'I have nothing to offer – no home, no impressive features. I would be starting from nothing here, working on land that belongs to another.'

Chanoch had tried to make himself useful to Set, getting stuck in with the farming that the others were doing. He knew enough to help and was a quick learner. But his back ached, and he was both grateful for the day of rest, and curious to see how his extended family celebrated it.

'Help me to honour you today, Yahweh, whatever the day looks like.'

When he arrived back at the main area of huts –
seven of them belonging to Adam, Set and their
immediate families, arranged in an almost-semi-circle –
around forty persons were gathered around the central
fire pit. Singing had begun. *Could that be—?*

It was. Shiphrah's back was to him, and she was
tapping a rhythm on a drum whilst singing praise to
Yahweh. Ima sat next to Shiphrah and led the tune, for it
was one she had composed. Chanoch wanted to show
Shiphrah he was there, to reach out and touch her
again, but instead he took a place on the opposite side
of the crowd and tried to blend in.

It didn't work. Shiphrah immediately saw him and
beamed from ear to ear. He couldn't help but smile
back. Had anyone noticed?

Shiphrah's lanky brother was there, along with
Yemima, who was sitting in Enosh's lap, with their
children gathered around their feet. The other families
sat the same way and Chanoch realised he'd positioned
himself in the midst of Raham's, rather close to one of
the beautiful daughters. This woman now turned her
head and batted her eyelashes at him. *She thinks my
smile is for her. How awkward!*

He turned his attention to the fire, hoping she
wouldn't think him rude, but not wanting to encourage
her.

The time of worship lasted well into the afternoon.
They sang more songs of praise, several people shared
stories old and new, Set taught a lesson about Yahweh,
and prayers were made for needs within the family. It
wasn't too dissimilar to what they might do at home,
just on a larger, more organised scale. However,
Chanoch noticed that unlike at home, many were

disengaged, and the children quickly became restless and began running around in the background. He also wondered why only half the valley dwellers had gathered for worship.

As soon as the circle broke for food, he approached Shiphrah. 'I'm pleased to see you,' he said, surprised by his own boldness.

'Oh? Did you miss me?' She spoke in jest, having no idea how much it was true.

'I did. Very much.'

'Oh,' she said again, her mouth dropping open.

Chanoch rubbed his beard and chuckled. 'How was your walk down here. Painful?'

Her mousy-coloured eyebrows drew together. 'You're the first person to ever ask me that. Yes, it was. But it was worth it. I love coming down for Shabbat. We don't do it each week, for we have to leave as soon as the sun rises, but Yemima was desperate to see Enosh, and I was happy to encourage the visit.'

'Oh?' He grinned at his mimic. 'Why was that?'

She brushed her fringe from her eyes and shrugged. 'I prefer the food down here. Ima is a better cook.' Then she pursed her lips, trying not to laugh.

He wanted to tickle her into submission, but he daren't do it, not with so many people around. 'Do you think you could manage walking further? Or could we find somewhere to sit away from the crowd?'

Shiphrah looked about and Chanoch followed her gaze. Everyone else was chatting, eating and paying little attention to them. 'Come with me,' she said.

She led him round to the rear of the huts. A well stood slightly off to the right-hand side, with a wooden construction next to it from which several water skins hung. Beside that was a small bench.

Chanoch helped Shiphrah to get comfortable, removing his outer garment for her to sit on, then perched next to her. They stared out at the arid plain that dominated the land to the east of the huts.

'Your abba dug this well,' Shiphrah said.

'He did?'

'And made the river dam that provides an area to soak our flax. Plus, he planted that tree—' she pointed far off towards the river, 'and that one, and that one. They give us plentiful figs each year.'

'How do you know all this?'

'Your ima told my abba the stories, and he has passed them on to me. Also, I chat to our grandfather whenever I can. He's not one to volunteer stories, but I can usually get him to talk if I goad him. The others don't realise Kayin did those things. They take them for granted…'

'They remember his awful actions…'

'And forget the good,' she finished. 'I know there are many sides to each person. No-one is all good or all bad. Even Shimon has redeeming features. I remember him and Channah teaching me to wield a sling when I was a tiny girl, before they disappeared from our lives. They said because I was vulnerable, I needed to know how to protect myself. No-one else ever thought to teach me.'

Chanoch felt the tap of her fingers on the bench and laid his hand over them. 'I'm pleased they showed you kindness. Yael said her mother still follows Yahweh.'

'Yael?'

Chanoch smiled, remembering the little blonde and her fiery temper. 'She captured me and dragged me at knife point to her mother. I think if she'd had her way, Ima and I would still be there, tied up, waiting for Shimon's judgement. She's a fair bit younger than us, so perhaps you never met her.'

'I haven't. She sounds like quite a character.'

He chuckled. 'She was. But beneath all her bluster, I think she had a good heart. Like you said, no-one is all bad.' He noticed Shiphrah was chewing her lip. 'What is it? What's the matter?'

With a visible effort, she lifted her eyes from her lap to meet his. 'You should be looking for someone like Yael. Someone strong and, I suspect, beautiful. You shouldn't be wasting your time with me.'

'But I like wasting time with you.' He squeezed her fingers, willing her to smile again.

She didn't. Instead, she pulled her hand away and struggled to standing. 'Don't do this, Chanoch. I was content before you came. I'd learnt to live at peace with my fate. Don't...'

'Shiphrah. Wait!' For she was walking away, back towards the crowd. What had he said? Why was she pushing him away?

Chanoch ran after her, but as he rounded the corner, he bumped into the girl who'd smiled at him earlier.

'Chanoch!' she exclaimed, dropping the food she'd been carrying.

'Forgive me.' He bent to retrieve her food, but it was covered in dust. She knew his name. He fought frantically to remember hers but could not. Embarrassed, he stood again. 'It's ruined. I'm sorry. Let me get you some more.'

'Thank you.'

Now he couldn't follow Shiphrah, who'd moved to Yemima's side and was refusing to glance his way. He must replace the other girl's food. She was still talking…

'I've been hoping for an opportunity to speak to you. Everyone keeps mentioning you.'

'They do?' he said, forcing his attention away from Shiphrah and onto the woman beside him.

'They say you've come from Nod. I've always wondered what it's like beyond the mountains. I wanted to go west with Uncle Nadav, but Abba wouldn't let me. He said I must marry first. But I don't want to marry anyone here.' This woman certainly knew her own mind. 'What's it like in Nod?'

Spying another basket of bread with a bowl of dried meat and fruit beside it, Chanoch apologised his way through the crowd to reach the food, with the young woman following.

'Well, it's similar to here,' he replied, selecting the best meat for her plate, 'though we have less waterways and it's slightly warmer. Just as here though, there's a wide variety of landscapes. We travel around depending on the season and the danger.'

'Is it really dangerous?' Her features lit up, and she placed a tiny portion of bread in her mouth.

'Sometimes. Though Yahweh protects us.'

She swallowed her minuscule mouthful. 'What's it like, living under a curse? Is it terribly exciting?'

What a strange thing to ask. 'No. Mostly inconvenient. But my father hasn't tested it since he returned to Yahweh.'

'Oh.' Her face fell as she rolled a grape in her fingers. 'My brothers also said you are here to find a wife.'

'Yes, among other things.' This was so awkward. Couldn't he just get to know someone without an expectation hanging over his head?

'What other things?'

'Hmm?'

'What other things are you here for?'

She was sharp and persistent. 'My mother wanted to see her family.'

'And is she enjoying herself?'

'Very much. Thank you for asking.' He looked at her in a new light. Perhaps she wasn't as self-consumed as she'd seemed at first. 'I'm very sorry, I've met so many people and I can't remember your name. It's rude of me…'

'Not at all. That's understandable. It's Talia.'

'A beautiful name.'

'Thank you. I think so too.'

'And, why don't you like any of the men here, Talia?'

'Because they are always leering, commenting and sometimes… touching. Especially Jared. I want someone kind, even if they aren't as good to look at.'

'Oh.' Was that comment aimed at him? 'I suppose that's… sensible?'

'So, tell me more about you. May we go for a walk?'

Chanoch insides crunched. While Talia's charm was increasingly interesting, he was unwilling to give Shiphrah the impression he would abandon her so readily. Fortunately, Talia seemed oblivious to the direction of his gaze. Was Shiphrah really so invisible?

'Come, Chanoch. My legs are aching for a walk after all that sitting. You will accompany me, won't you? I don't feel safe going alone.'

That got his attention. Was that her objective, or could it be true that she didn't feel safe? 'Of course. Shall we go to the river?'

Talia beamed and offered him her arm. Unsure what else to do, Chanoch held his out too, which she quickly grabbed and threaded hers through. 'You are funny. Are you so unused to women?' she laughed, as they began striding towards the river.

'Entirely.' Despite his best intentions, he smiled, and Talia beamed at him again. Sunlight highlighted the tendrils of curly hair falling over her perfectly contoured face. She really was very beautiful. 'Where I come from, the only other women are my sisters and mother.'

'That must be terrible. No wonder you are desperate for a wife.'

I wasn't, but here I am anyway.

'Do you think your father would accept me, a murderer's son?' Chanoch almost kicked himself. Why had he said that? Rejection was at the forefront of his mind, but Talia might take such comments as a proposal.

'I can work on him, if that's what you want,' she said, running her tongue over her lip. 'And then I can live with you, instead of in this retched place.'

She *had* taken it as a proposal. Chanoch should use this opportunity to correct her thinking, to explain that he was meant to stay between the rivers, but his mind went blank as a life with Talia flashed into his imagination.

I can't do this, Yahweh. Help me!

Suddenly, a scream came from the river. Dropping Talia's arm, Chanoch sprinted towards it. A child struggled in the water, bobbing up and down, barely staying afloat. Chanoch went to strip his outer garment and realised he'd left it on the bench by the well. He dove into the water.

Never in his life had he been so grateful for the constant swimming lessons his abba insisted on. He reached the child with ease, wrapped his arms around her chest and dragged her backwards until they were safely on the bank. Then he patted and rubbed her back, encouraging her to expel all the water she'd swallowed.

Talia threw herself to her knees and enveloped the child in an embrace. 'You saved my little sister!' she exclaimed. 'You saved her life. Oh, Chanoch, how can I ever repay you?' And she flung herself onto his chest, weeping.

SET

Chanoch tried to see Shiphrah again that Shabbat, but she kept evading him. The following day, he went back out to the fields. He stayed close to Set all week, preferring the solemn man's company to that of his peers. Inspired by Shiphrah, he asked Set to tell him stories about the area and about Yahweh.

Set looked pleased with the request and happily talked as they worked. Mid-morning on the fifth day, Set had an idea. 'Come with me. We'll walk around the boundaries of the land, and you can see if anything takes your fancy.'

'Takes my fancy?'

'There are still some uncultivated areas. Perhaps something will catch your eye as a suitable site for raising your own family.' So Ima had confessed to her brother that she intended to leave him here. It made Chanoch feel better. Hopefully he wouldn't have to deal with the assumption that he was returning to Nod any longer – though where would that leave him with Talia?

Better she knows sooner rather than later. Then she can reject me if she chooses. The thought lightened Chanoch's step. Any normal man would be thrilled at Talia's interest. Why had it caused him tension?

Because of Shiphrah. Of course, he knew that was the reason, but he'd been trying to talk himself out of it. Why did being with Talia feel like betraying Shiphrah, even though he'd promised Shiphrah nothing, and she didn't seem to want him?

As he strode through the fields with Set, pulling up stray weeds as they went, he wondered if he should speak to this man about his daughter. Set got in there first.

'So… you've been here a while. Have you had any thoughts about your future?'

Chanoch gulped.

'You don't have to answer. I didn't mean to pressure you. I just noticed you with Talia the other day, and Enosh mentioned Sarai.

'I haven't even spoken to Sarai,' he said quickly. 'Sorry, I know she's your daughter. But that was entirely Enosh's suggestion.'

'No offence taken. But Talia?'

'We spoke for the first time on Shabbat. She is… nice.'

Set raised an eyebrow. 'Most men in our clan are head over heels in love with her. I take it you are not?'

Chanoch stopped walking to pull at a stubborn weed. 'I don't know her well enough to say. She's beautiful, but looks aren't everything.'

Set smiled, and they continued up a slight incline towards the forest. 'You know, when I was young I wasn't particularly interested in women. I devoted myself to learning – about the crops, about the past and about Yahweh. I preferred being with your mother than anyone my own age because she was sensible, and all the other girls seemed shallow. The fact you've stuck by my side all week suggests you might be similar.'

'I suppose so. I can't deny I've been interested in meeting others beyond my own family, but it hasn't been compulsive. I was happy in Nod before coming here. Ima would have made the journey sooner if I'd shown interest. Abba often pokes fun at my lack of ambition – I'm quite the opposite of what he was like. I prefer to get on with things in quietness. I suppose I've seen the battle Abba has to keep his will in line with Yahweh's, and I've been grateful that my will is not so strong.'

'Yes. You certainly favour your mother in temperament. Not that I ever met your abba, of course. Though I feel like I know him through the stories.'

'Stories you've relayed to Shiphrah.'

Set stopped in surprise. 'You've been talking to Shiphrah?'

Chanoch felt his cheeks warming. This was the opening he'd been looking for, yet now it was here, he feared to walk through it. 'We spent some time together at Yemima's house.'

'And she spoke to you?'

'She took a little encouragement.' His mouth twitched into a half-smile. 'But we soon got on. Well, in fact. Except that on Shabbat—'

'Go on...'

'I don't know if I've offended her, but we were talking by the well, then all of a sudden, she got up and left. She said I shouldn't be wasting my time with her and that she was content before I came. I don't know what she meant!'

'Ah.' Set sighed and sat down on a large root protruding beneath a huge oak tree. 'Did you know that we nearly lost her once?'

Chanoch nodded.

'It was her eighth winter. She'd had a terrible fit and banged her head on a rock. Blood gushed forth from it, and although we got to her quickly and bound her head, she fell asleep and stayed that way for many days. My wife stayed by her side the entire time, and I joined her whenever I could. She looked so helpless – our poor little girl, in a blood-stained tunic and bandages, with erratic breathing and lips as dry as cracked earth.'

A tear came into Set's eye. 'I thought we were going to lose her. But Yahweh showed mercy. We sacrificed our best lamb and he devoured the offering. By nightfall, she had begun to stir. When she woke, I vowed to care for her better. She stayed by my side for many years, coming to the fields with me daily. She was never afraid of trying to help, but constantly became frustrated that her body allowed her to do so little. I tried to protect her – perhaps too much. I didn't want her doing herself any damage.'

'That is understandable,' Chanoch said.

'When Yemima asked if Shiphrah could move in with her, I resisted. I was determined to keep my little girl within my sight. But by then, she wasn't a little girl. She had seen forty summers and had no family of her own. My wife convinced me to let her go, saying it would give Shiphrah more purpose, more meaning to her life. She was right of course, and Shiphrah has thrived up in the hills, though she wishes I hadn't sent her little brother to *constantly* protect her.' He grinned.

'I'm telling you all this because… I am probably partly responsible. Responsible for why she doesn't believe any man could be interested in her. She thinks she has no value, except as a help to her sister. I'm not sure whether no man approached her because I was in the way, or because of her disabilities, but the fact is, she doesn't see who she is.'

'She is special,' Chanoch confirmed.

'But is she special enough for you to marry her?' Set asked with a penetrating gaze. 'Because, Chanoch, if you are just toying with her, then I don't want you anywhere near her. You don't need to tell me Shiphrah has inner beauty – I know that well enough – but when placed against someone like Talia…? You are still a man with flesh, blood, and all the passions that come with it.'

Chanoch rubbed his beard, considering Set's words. He was grateful for them, and not offended. It was right to be having this conversation. It was right to consider the depth of his feelings and all future possibilities. Yet when he considered the future, he couldn't see one with Talia in it. Whereas Shiphrah? He saw her surrounded by a gaggle of children – his children. He saw her in his arms at night, a strand of unruly, mousy hair blowing up and falling down as she breathed in peaceful slumber. He saw her with him in Nod, watching the sunset on his favourite hill, tending little gardens they planted together, meeting his abba and enjoying an evening making jokes at his expense. He *saw* her.

But she couldn't come to Nod. Besides the fact he was meant to stay between the rivers, Shiphrah would never manage the journey. But if he stayed here and married her, might there always be the temptation of other women? Was Set wise to point out that he was still a man, with earthly passions?

Undoubtedly.

'What are you thinking?' Set asked.

Saliva rose in his throat, and Chanoch had to gulp it down. 'It is still very early to say this, but I think I love Shiphrah. I think I have have loved her from the moment I heard her sing on the hillside. But I do not want to hurt her.'

Set nodded and put an arm on his shoulder. 'Then I suggest you find a way of letting Talia down as soon as possible. She is too good a woman to be second choice, and she would never accept it. As for Shiphrah, there is no rush for you to marry, and you are welcome to stay with my family as long as you like. Take your time, and seek Yahweh's will.'

They continued their walk around the grounds in comfortable silence. Chanoch was grateful for his uncle's wisdom and kindness, and Set seemed content to be quiet. Chanoch didn't see any land that caught his eye, though he wasn't paying it a great deal of attention.

Just before they arrived at the huts, Chanoch asked a final question. 'If I did desire to marry your daughter, and I assured you of my undivided affection, would you have any objection to me – in principle?'

Set's brows drew together. 'I'm not sure what you mean.'

'I am Kayin's son. Even if I favour my mother, his blood runs in me.'

'I see.' Set paused, then lifted both his hands and placed them on Chanoch's shoulders. 'My mother,

Chavah, was the first to believe the deceiver's hiss. She broke the bond with Yahweh, and we all suffer for it. But had I been in that situation, had I been tempted by those words, I cannot say for sure that I wouldn't have done the same. So, I do not blame her for my suffering, nor blame her for my sin. I am my own person, responsible for my own choices.

'So it is with you, Chanoch. Your abba is paying the price for what he did every day that he walks in his judgement. Every day he stays in Nod, unable to see his family, unable to farm, and hunted by Shimon. Because you have lived with him, you have so far lived with that. But it is not your future. You are your own person, and it is time to stop walking in your father's judgement. As for my daughter, I am far more concerned with whether her future husband trusts Yahweh than whether he comes from the right bloodline. Do you trust Yahweh, Chanoch?'

'My trust is not faultless,' Chanoch confessed. 'But I am trying.'

'That is more than many are doing. And the good thing is, Yahweh doesn't require much of our trust. If you keep your heart soft, and your ears open, you are halfway there.'

CONFESSIONS

Chanoch took a while to go to sleep that night. He spent much time praying, asking for wisdom as Set had requested. By the time he fell asleep, he knew what he must do in the morning, but he wasn't looking forward to it.

He sought Talia out immediately. *Better to get it over with.* She waved as he approached, and he was pleased to see she was at a loom with her sister nearby. That meant they wouldn't need to be alone together but could still talk privately. He sat crossed-legged on the ground next to her.

'I'm glad you've come. I was beginning to think you were avoiding me,' she said.

'No, just working. Although, in truth, I haven't known what to say until this morning.'

'Oh? You must mean about how I can repay you. I was wondering what you'd ask for.' Talia batted her eyelashes and leaned forward slightly.

'No. Not that. You don't owe me anything. I am just pleased I was in the right place at the right time to save your sister. The alternative is unthinkable.'

'Indeed. Poor little mite. Though I should *like* to repay you.'

Chanoch ignored her grin. Strangely, her teasing was making it easier for him to say what he needed to. It may attract other men, but it didn't entice him. *I prefer Shiphrah in every possible way.*

'Talia, I came to speak with you because you deserve to know the truth.'

She raised a single eyebrow and sat back slightly.

'I am privileged to have met you and flattered that you would ever consider me a suitor… I'm not wrong, am I? That is what you meant?' he asked, realising he didn't want to embarrass either of them unnecessarily.

Talia, uncharacteristically bashful, shook her head. 'You're not wrong.'

'I think you will make someone a wonderful wife, but not me. For my heart already belongs to another.'

'It does? Then what was that about asking my father?'

'I'm sorry; it slipped out. I hadn't meant to say it, and it wasn't what I meant. I feel terrible for leading you in the wrong direction…I-I…'

A small smile crept onto Talia's lips and she reached out a single hand, placing it on his arm. 'It's alright, Chanoch. I am hardly in love with you, and you aren't breaking my heart or anything. I just liked the fact you were different. You were the only man who hadn't come begging, and honestly, it was refreshing.'

Chanoch exhaled and smiled. *That was easier than I thought. Thank you, Yahweh, for providing this opportunity and not letting it drag on.*

'So, who is she?' Talia asked.

'What?'

'Who does your heart belong to?'

'Oh. I-I'd rather not say just now. I don't know if she feels the same way yet.'

'I hope she does. I'll pray for you.'

That was surprising. Talia constantly surprised him. 'Thank you. I'd appreciate that.'

As Talia continued her work on the loom, running her delicate fingers expertly over and under the fibres, Chanoch wondered for a brief moment whether he'd made a mistake.

No. You made the way. I will trust You.

Next he sought out Set, who conveniently was having breakfast with his ima.

'I'd like your permission to visit Yemima's household for a few days. I assume they won't be coming down for Shabbat tomorrow?'

'I doubt it. Enosh went back yesterday. You're welcome to go, not that you need my permission,' Set replied.

'Do you mind, Ima?'

'Not at all, my love. Though I'd rather stay here. Can you remember the way?'

'Yes, I believe so.'

'Chanoch.' Set glanced over at Talia, just visible outside the furthest hut. 'Have you done what we discussed?'

'I have. It went well.'

Set smiled and Ima nudged him in the ribs. 'Don't tell me you two have secrets I'm not privy to. He is my son, not yours, *brother*.'

'He might be mine soon,' Set chuckled under his breath.

Ima raised her eyebrows. 'Does that mean what I think it does?'

'Maybe,' Chanoch interjected. 'I don't know yet whether she'll accept me. But I would at least like the opportunity to get to know her better. Even if nothing comes of it.'

Ima jumped up and wrapped him in her arms. 'I'm proud of you,' she whispered in his ear.

'I had a good example to follow. You didn't exactly choose the easy option, did you Ima?'

'It doesn't matter whether an option is easy or difficult. It matters whether it is Yahweh's will. Seek that, and you cannot go too far wrong.'

'I am seeking it, Ima.'

After gathering a water-skin and a change of clothes, Chanoch left, following the path they'd taken on the way down. It wasn't hard to see where to go. Sheep droppings littered the well-worn way, and the hill-country dominated the distance, a marker for the journey.

Without sheep to hold him back, it was much quicker even with the uphill climb, and when the sun was at its peak, he saw her. Shiphrah was hanging laundry on the branches of a tree, struggling to reach all but the lowest ones. Her hair was loose, blowing in the gentle breeze that crested the hill.

'Let me help you.' Chanoch ran up and took a blanket off her, shook it out and threw it over a higher branch. He wasn't much taller than her, but tall enough.

'What are you doing here?' she exclaimed. 'I thought...'

Chanoch wasn't going to let her brush him off again. He immediately took her hands and held them tightly. 'I want to know you better. To know your hopes and longings that you've never dared confess to anyone else. I want to spend time with you – imagining stories in the clouds, telling our own tales or… or doing nothing in particular! I want to feel what freedom is. Freedom to be myself without living in anyone's shadow, freedom to sing, cry and praise with no inhibition, freedom to love under no expectation. I want to see you as you see me. For you do… don't you?'

Shiphrah stood, mouth open.

'Did I say too much?' he asked.

A smile tugged at her lips. 'Have you ever said so much without stopping before?'

'Probably not.'

'Should I be concerned or flattered?'

He squeezed her fingers, refusing to drop his gaze. 'Just tell me you feel it too. Tell me that I'm not imagining this.'

Shiphrah pulled a hand away. His chest tightened. Was she going to leave? But then she lifted her hand up and brushed his cheek. 'I thought once you met the other women you would forget about me. I thought you'd consider me as a friend, or even like a sister, but I never thought… I never hoped… No one has looked at me like this before, Chanoch. The way you are looking at me now.'

'That's because they are all blind.'

She shook her head. 'No. They see the truth. It is you that are blind.'

She tried to tug her other hand away, but he refused to release her. 'Shiphrah, I love you. I don't care if you have physical limitations; the strength of your heart makes up for them in abundance.'

'You say that now, but how will you feel when I am next sick? How will you feel if I can't have children? How will you feel when you are lumbered with a wife who cannot care for you as you grow old, but whom you must care for – for who knows how many years? Hundreds? Thousands? I cannot ask you to do that, Chanoch!'

'You're not asking me to. And I'm not asking you to either. I'm just asking for a few days, Shiphrah. A few days without expectation. Forget about what everyone else thinks a family should and shouldn't look like. Forget about what people have spoken over you in the past. Let's take a few days to get to know one another and then… and then we can discuss those things if you want to. Only if you want to.'

Shiphrah took a step closer and her arms finally relaxed. Chanoch longed to gather her into his, to hold her and not let go, but he would not break his word. No expectation.

'Alright. We have today, and tomorrow is Shabbat. After that, I don't know…'

'Take as much time as you need.' The voice came from behind him and Chanoch turned to see Yemima standing, watching. How long had she been there? She walked towards them and placed a hand on her niece's back.

'Shiphrah. Enosh said he'll be home for a while. I can manage without you watching the children. This is more important. You must not refuse this opportunity. I shall not allow it.'

A REQUEST

I want to marry you.'

It was a week later, and Chanoch had barely left Shiphrah's side. She'd proven all his instincts correct, and, as they stood beneath the same tree he'd declared himself under, gazing out over the valley below where sheep dotted the rugged landscape and the far-off Tigris glinted in the sunlight, Shiphrah consented.

The words hung in the air, heavy with emotion and promise. 'But I have a request.'

'You do?' Chanoch gathered her into his arms, barely believing that they were having this conversation. She did not resist him, nor did he wonder whether he needed permission. Over the past few days, they'd become comfortable in each other's presence, and he no longer doubted either his affection or hers. When he'd simply asked to spend time with her, he'd genuinely meant it. If she'd taken four seasons to declare her love, he'd have enjoyed every moment of the wait. But she hadn't. She loved him and she knew it, and all she'd needed was reassurance that she was worthy of being loved herself.

Now she felt secure enough to request something of him. Anticipation gathered in his abdomen as he gazed into her almond-eyes, longing to kiss her and know for the first time what it felt like.

'I want you to take me away with you.'

Chanoch jolted back in surprise, but did not release her. 'What?'

She leaned forward, closing the gap between them again, and settled her head upon his chest. 'I have lived my entire life in this place. I love my family and do not resent that, but I long to see the world. I want to see what Nod is like before I am too frail and I can no longer cope with the journey.'

'What makes you think you'll be too frail in the future? Is your condition worsening?' They had already had extensive conversations about what she could and couldn't do, where she felt pain and what that pain felt like. She hadn't mentioned it getting better or worse, only that she was susceptible to disease and must be careful around anyone who was sick.

'No. I don't think so. But I'd rather not risk living with regrets. I know you had planned to stay between the rivers, but I also know you'd rather go home. The bond with your parents is strong, and they are all you have. You haven't grown up surrounded by steadily multiplying people like I have. You haven't experienced loss. Whereas every few years, another family leaves the land between the rivers, and I've grown used to it. I've learnt how to say goodbye.'

'I.. but… what about your mother and father?'

'I haven't lived with them for ten years. I've been up here with Yemima and, truly, there are plenty of others who can do what I do. I'm not denying it will be hard for me to leave, but it will be harder for you to stay.'

Hope flickered in Chanoch's heart, hope that he might see his homeland again and might see Abba again. He shouldn't indulge it. They had agreed he would stay; that was what he was meant to do, wasn't it? Besides…

'How will you manage the journey? It is not easy crossing the mountains and there are many predators.'

'We can take our time, going slowly, as your ima did the first time she crossed them. If we need to stop, we stop. There's no rush to be anywhere. We can simply waste time together.' As she looked up at him, her smile as bright as the sunlight, his heart leapt in his chest.

He exhaled, feeling the warmth of her skin as he touched his forehead to hers. *What do I say, Yahweh? Can this be Your will, after all? Didn't You want me to stay here?*

A tickle caressed his lips. Then Shiphrah was kissing him, gently and slowly, but with the same hunger he'd been trying to contain. The sensation in his chest spread all over his body and it almost felt like he was flying, joining the pictures in the clouds.

When she pulled away, his smile spread wide and he could barely keep from laughing. 'You are wonderful.'

'I love you, Chanoch.'

A chuckle escaped. 'I would hope so, after doing that.'

'So, will you take me to Nod?'

'I don't have peace about it yet, but I will speak with Ima. Will that do for now?'

She snuggled back into his arms. 'It will do for now.'

They spent a few more days in the hill country, praying and praising together, before Chanoch decided he must return to the valley to talk with Ima and Set.

Leaving Shiphrah behind was like a spear to the heart and as he walked away, back down the hill, he wondered how he'd ever lived without her.

Set approached as soon as he saw him. 'How did it go?'

Chanoch couldn't prevent himself from grinning.

'That well, huh?' Set laughed. 'So, are you here to seek my permission to marry my daughter?'

'Yes, but there is something else.'

'Do tell.'

'I'd like to speak with Ima as well. Can we all get together tonight?' He realised Shiphrah should have come too; it made more sense for her to explain what was sure to shock her father, and Chanoch wished he'd thought of that before. He'd been concerned about sparing her a painful journey, but that concern seemed obsolete considering her request involved a far longer one.

'Certainly. Let's talk after the evening meal.' When Chanoch moved to pick up a tool, Set stopped him. 'There's no need for you to work today. Go and enjoy the company of others.'

Feeling slightly like he'd been rebuffed, Chanoch made his way towards the huts and was pleased to see Ima outside with her mother, cooking. Chanoch had barely spent any time with Chavah, and now that he might be leaving the land between the rivers, he felt the pressure of time on these new relationships. Should he try to develop them, or just leave them be?

There was nothing stilted in the interactions between the two women. It was almost like Ima had never left. When she saw him, Ima immediately ran to embrace him before returning to Chavah.

'Can I help with anything?' Chanoch asked.

'I'm sure you need to sit down after your walk,' Chavah replied. 'Here, have some tea.'

She passed him some hot, mint-infused water, and he sat on a small wicker stool by the fire-pit.

'Was you time at Yemima's fruitful?' Ima asked.

'Yes, but I'd like to discuss it later with Set. I've arranged for us to meet after dinner.'

'Very well. This sounds mysterious.'

'Not mysterious; we just need your wisdom.'

'How are you settling into our land?' Chavah asked him. 'I expect it's taken some adjustment.'

It was a pertinent question. What should he say – *I like it well enough, but I might be leaving?* 'It is lovely, and I've been made very welcome, for which I'm grateful.'

'But...?' Chavah waited for him to elaborate.

'I'm not sure I've quite settled.'

'You probably won't until you have a space to call your own. I remember the years I wandered with Adam outside Eden; we never settled until we stopped here, built our home and started a family.'

'I've never known a permanent home, though. The whole land east of the mountains holds memories for me, yet it is the people I lived with that were home, rather than any particular place. Abba, Ima and my siblings.'

'How is my eldest son?' Chavah asked. 'I've heard from Awan's lips of course, but your perspective will be different. Is he a good father?' She spoke with a smile, putting Chanoch back at ease. He was glad she hadn't probed further into the previous conversation.

'He is the best abba, though of course, I have little to compare him to. He gets grumpy sometimes, but who wouldn't? My younger sisters can be quite infuriating.' Chanoch's laugh betrayed his lack of seriousness. 'I miss him. I miss our talks around the fire, our little experiments and the way he teases me without ever being unkind. I wish he could have come with us and seen you all again.'

The same expression that so often graced his ima's face settled on his grandmother's. 'I wish it too,' she said. 'Even so, it would not be wise.'

'Chavah isn't any different to anyone else,' Chanoch said later as Set joined them in front of the fire. He was continuing a conversation with Ima about her mother.

'Of course she isn't. Did you expect her to be?' Ima asked.

'Well, she walked with Yahweh Elohim in the Garden. She knows what that was like.'

'But there have been many, many winters since then, and life continues as it always has since the banishment. We cannot live in the past, Chanoch, but must always move forwards.'

'I too wish I knew what that was like,' Set said. 'Perhaps the longing in all of us to seek something better stems from the knowledge, deep inside, that we were created for greater things. Perhaps we are destined to be eternally dissatisfied.'

'Not eternally,' Ima said. 'For satisfaction can be found in Yahweh, if we will seek Him to a greater extent than we seek what is outside of Him. And, though we don't know how long our lives are, we know He put a limit on them when our parents decided that seizing the knowledge of good and evil was better than trusting Yahweh to provide it.'

'Is that what happened at the tree?' Set asked.

'I believe so. At least, in my experience, knowledge of what is good comes from intimately knowing the One who is good. There are no shortcuts. If we seek a quicker route to knowledge, we fall short of His design for us.'

'So it was always about having a relationship with Him, not about following rules, or what we do,' Set said.

'Yes, but what we do still reflects what is in our heart.'

'Speaking of the heart and seeking better things, that is what I wanted to discuss.' Two sets of eyes settled on Chanoch, and he could no longer delay telling them. 'Shiphrah and I would like to marry, but she has made an unexpected request. She wants me to take her to Nod.'

Their shock was apparent. 'I'm not sure how I feel about it. I was getting used to the idea of staying, though my heart longs for home, and I cannot deny that the idea of Shiphrah making the journey terrifies me.'

Ima looked at Set, waiting for him to speak, but her brother leaned forward and put his head in his hands, rubbing his hair between his fingers.

'We always assumed you would stay here. The words of Yahweh Elohim, when He presented Ima to Abba, were that a man should leave his father and mother and be united with his wife,' Ima said.

Set spoke next. 'However, this may be more about the fact he must put his wife first – she becomes his primary focus – than about where they live. For we are all commanded to multiply, and to do that, we must spread over the earth.'

'Yet, I also suspect that having the man leave protects the woman. She will need the aid of her mother and sisters when she has her own children, and if she becomes part of the man's family instead, there is the potential for her to be valued less.'

'How so?' Set asked.

'This may not occur to you, brother, humble as you are. But think for a moment of Shimon and Channah. Channah wants to follow Yahweh; she wants to live in harmony with her siblings. Yet, she is bound by her husband to live a separate life, set against those she loves. She does not have the physical strength to stand up to him, nor the strength of will. And so, he wins.

'Now imagine a more powerful man than Shimon doing the same thing. Imagine he has many sons and they all stay within his household and bring their wives into it. Wouldn't tyranny soon reign within that home? Whereas if each of the sons was bound to give up his status, to leave his parents and cleave to his wife – dedicating himself to putting her needs and wants above his father's – it breaks the cycle. Each family begins afresh, each woman is valued for her own sake rather than what she can contribute to the father's ambition.'

'You have far-reaching eyes, Awan. I see only our little collection of families between the rivers, but you seem to see beyond, into a future I don't recognise,' Set said.

'Perhaps I am allowing my imagination to run away with me. Still, I live with a man who did great evil once, which uniquely places me to understand how quickly people can sink into something unrecognisable. Men are physically stronger than women. What will happen if they one day decide to abuse that strength?'

Set ran his hands through his hair again. 'I hope I never live to see that day. However, I think we need to pull things back to the present in order to consider my daughter's request. I am with you, Chanoch. The thought of Shiphrah making that journey fills me with dread, and yet I know in my heart that she has always longed to see more of the world. This place is bound up with people's expectations of her, or lack of them. So, her request is not altogether surprising; it is something I have long feared.'

'Nor do I want to lose you, Chanoch, you know that,' Ima said, extending her hand towards him. 'Yet my conviction stands. I came here ready to entrust you into Set's care, and I still believe that is for the best. You and Shiphrah may travel – perhaps go on short journeys – but your home should be here where you are safe, and where Yahweh's people are. I cannot stress enough how hard it is to live alone.'

'But Awan,' Set interjected. 'Imagine if you were in Shiphrah's situation? Indeed, you we were once. For you left this place and went after Kayin, claiming that Yahweh called you to do it. Don't you think you're being inconsistent, saying she should not leave? Besides, Chanoch doesn't seem like the type to enforce his will on my daughter.'

Chanoch hadn't expected Set to be his primary advocate, and as he sat spectator in this argument about his life and future, he didn't know which opinion made the most sense, or even where his heart lay. *Yahweh, help me.*

Don't be afraid. I am here.

'I don't think we should have had this conversation without Shiphrah present,' Chanoch said at last. 'It was a mistake for me to come here without her. Would you both be willing to return to the hills tomorrow and speak with us together?'

Ima and Set exchanged a meaningful glance and a nod.

'Wherever you live,' Set said, 'I would be pleased to call you my son, Chanoch. We haven't even mentioned that, but truly, I am thrilled you have chosen Shiphrah, and she has chosen you.' Tears welled in his eyes. 'I never thought I'd see her wed, and for her to find a man that values her so much...' He knelt in front of Chanoch. 'Thank you, my son.'

Chanoch found himself lost for words, for he hadn't done anything worthy of commendation. He had simply fallen in love. 'I will do my best to care for her as long as I live.'

'I know you will.'

ATTACK

Chanoch's legs ached when he woke at sunrise, but he stretched them out, telling them they mustn't complain, for they had more work to do that day. An uphill climb awaited.

They set off as soon as Set had given instructions to his workers, enabling them to get on without him.

'Do you think Kayin could come for the wedding?' Set asked, as he hopped over a stone wall designed to keep the sheep in.

'Oh no,' Ima replied. 'Abba said we must stay clear of Shimon, and if Kayin himself should come—'

'You're right. I wish I could meet him though.'

Ima grinned. 'He's always intrigued you. You constantly goaded me for stories when you were young.'

'You were good at telling them. Tell me what he's like presently. I can't help being curious about the brother I've never met.'

So Ima did. As they ventured through the forest, she told of Kayin's transformation when she met him, the eventual confession and acceptance of his fate, and of

Yahweh's extraordinary mercy. 'Never doubt that Yahweh loves us, Set. No matter what.'

After they left the shaded woods and the mid-morning sun warmed their faces again, they saw the hill country up ahead. Set and Ima were still chatting when the urge to run seized Chanoch. He wondered where Shiphrah would be – at the brook, playing with the children outside the hut, or further up, lying on the grass staring at the clouds?

'Don't fail me now,' he muttered, urging his legs to comply with the jog. 'Shiphrah!' he called, not expecting an answer, for she was unlikely to be this far down, but desperate to hear her voice.

When he had jogged further and the hut was in sight, but still far off, he called again. 'Shiphrah! Where are you?'

Then he heard the scream. Faint and short, like it was stopped midway through. *Was* it a scream? Could it have been an owl screeching? No, surely not. What owl screeches at the high point of the sun?

'Shiphrah?' He stopped running and listened more carefully. Nothing. Surely he'd imagined it? Yet, something in his gut told him he had not.

Chanoch squeezed his eyes shut, concentrating. *Yahweh, help me.* Something even fainter, like a muffled cry, came from his left. Opening his eyes, he adjusted course and sprinted. 'Shiphrah!'

It was inconceivable, her being attacked. Who would do it, so close to her home? And why? Yet even the faintest possibility spurred him on. Perhaps it was a wild animal? No. A wild animal couldn't muffle its prey.

More desperate now, he shouted her name over and over, stopping to listen, then running further into the small patch of woods. No more hints. No more clues. Nothing. Still, he ran, jumping over stones and roots. *Where is she, Yahweh?*

'Chano—!'

He spun. That came from behind him.

Spying a thicket some one-hundred strides away, he pushed forward. If she's not here, she could be in there.

Something moved within it, then a figure ducked out and ran, not glancing his way but pelting in the opposite direction.

Should he follow?

A wail arose from inside the bushes. Chanoch reached them and crawled through.

Shiphrah.

She lay on the floor, holding her head at an odd angle. Her tunic was above her knees. On seeing him, tears poured, creating rivulets of dirty water on her muddied cheeks. As she removed her hand from her head, reaching towards him, her fingers were scarlet.

'My love! No...'

Chanoch pulled her into his arms and held her, loosening his grip when she flinched. As he buried his face in her neck, he caught the scent of grass and fear. 'What happened?'

Shiphrah did not speak, but her shoulders raised and lowered as sobs racked her body. Pulling his face away from her neck, Chanoch pondered her. 'Shiphrah...?'

Tears blurred his vision, obscuring his beloved, but he saw enough. Her eyelids closed, her head flopped to one side, and her full weight sank into his arms.

Aftermath

Chanoch held vigil by Shiphrah's bed. After carrying her back to the hut and laying her there, he did not move all that day. For she slept fitfully, murmuring in her sleep, tossing and turning, her face creasing with pain as her body involuntarily spasmed. By the time Set and Awan arrived and discerned the situation, Yemima had cleaned Shiphrah's wound and bound it.

'How did you find her?' Set asked, placing a hand on Chanoch's arm.

It took some moments for Chanoch to realise Set was there, and when he peeled his gaze from Shiphrah's wounded face, he met her father's, full of all the concern he felt.

'She was in a thicket. She screamed for me. Someone did this to her… someone…'

'How do you know it was a person?' Set asked.

'I saw someone. And…' Chanoch averted his eyes from Shiphrah's body. 'Look at her legs.'

He knew what Set would see – bruises on her thighs – but she didn't deserve the indignity of his scrutiny.

When he heard Set replace the bed covering and felt the tension of his silence, he turned back.

Set's face was straight and stern, but his nostrils flared. 'Wh-who would do this?'

With a frustrated shake of his head, Chanoch let out a heavy sigh. The retreating figure had been too far away to recognise. They wouldn't know until Shiphrah woke. She would wake, wouldn't she? *Yahweh, help us.*

Set rose and left the hut, and Chanoch heard his anger let loose outside – a thrown jar, a howl, a gasp and wail as someone, likely Ima, held him tightly. Then Chanoch felt another enter the room. He let his eyelids close, needing no sight to recognise the presence.

Do not fear. I am here.

How could You let this happen?

There was no further answer, but an arm of love wrapped around him until he could do nothing but lower his face onto the blanket covering Shiphrah's legs and weep.

Chanoch fell asleep there. When he next woke, it was pitch black, but he heard Ima's gentle snore beside him and Shiphrah's breathing – steadier than it had been before. *She lives. Thank You.*

Dawn brought a whimper. Chanoch's eyes flickered open. A sliver of light inside the hut cast a faint glow on Shiphrah's face, just enough to make out her profile. He shuffled over until his face was level with hers. 'Are you awake, love?'

A groan.

Water.

He pulled himself to standing and tiptoed carefully around Ima's sleeping form, then over Set's. After pushing aside the linen hanging that separated Shiphrah's quarters from Yemima's, he crept past his aunt's sleeping children, through the doorway, and outside.

'I think she's waking,' he said to Yemima, who had a water-skin hung on her shoulder. She must have just returned from the brook.

'Take this,' she replied, pressing it into his hand. 'I'll bring something to eat directly.'

When he reached Shiphrah's side, she stirred. 'Chanoch, is that you?'

'I have water,' he replied. 'Can you sit up a little?'

Ima heard and came immediately to Shiphrah's other side, supporting her back. Shiphrah glugged the water, wiped her mouth and allowed it to turn up in a weak smile.

'What do you have to smile about?' Chanoch asked, his voice breaking. He longed to kiss her, to confirm that she was real.

'You saved me.'

As he shook his head, a tear escaped Chanoch's eye, splashing onto the dusty floor. 'It wasn't enough.'

'It was. You came at just the right moment.'

'You mean…?'

'Jared did not succeed.'

'Jared?' The growl came from behind them and when Chanoch turned, Set's face was red and his teeth bared. He stood, fists clenched and strode from the room. Ima followed.

'Set—'

Chanoch could hear them through the mud walls. He held Shiphrah's hand and stroked it, not knowing what else to do.

'I must find him. I will—'

'Set, do not allow thoughts of vengeance to take root in your mind.' It was Ima.

'I can't do nothing!'

'Consider Shimon. He allowed those roots to grow deep and now the lives of an entire family are consumed by it. That must not be your fate.'

'I must still find him. Jared cannot be left to repeat the offence.'

'Yes, he must be found, but not by you. Either he'll have fled last night, expecting Shiphrah to have told all, or he'll be biding his time, waiting to see what occurs. Either way, you cannot lead the charge; you are too likely to do something you'll regret.'

'I will go to the valley, Abba.' It was Enosh's voice. 'I will find out where he is, and if he's there, I will gather several men to capture him. If he has fled, we will soon know it.'

'How angry are you, Enosh?' Ima asked.

'I am in control. Besides, Jared is… was my friend. He will be more likely to speak to me than Abba. I can get his side of the story.'

'His side of the—? How can you say that? How could there be another side? Your sister is undoubtedly innocent! We've all seen the way Jared looks at women.'

'Yes, Abba. I'm not suggesting otherwise. I'm just saying… Never mind. I will leave now; the sooner the better.'

'Take your eldest son with you,' Ima said. 'He can run back with a message if need be. But Set – you are staying here.'

Moments later, Set was back beside Shiphrah. Chanoch was pleased to see he'd calmed somewhat, although his next question didn't bode well.

'Will you tell me what happened?'

'Will you promise not to kill him?' Shiphrah said, her eyes pools of pity.

'Ah!' Set leaned forwards, kissed her head, then stroked her cheek. 'I always thought I was a sensible man, not given to violent passions.'

'That's not what I've heard,' Shiphrah replied, her mouth twitching.

'What have you heard?'

'That you married Ima really quickly.' Shiphrah giggled.

Set looked as though he was pretending to be shocked, then gave in and laughed. 'Fair enough. That much is true, I suppose. How can you be like this in the face of what has happened? How are you so calm?'

'Because Yahweh answered my prayers, Abba. I'm not denying I was scared, and my head really hurts, but it could have been so much worse. Saying that…'

'What?' Set brushed her cheek again. 'Speak, my love.'

Shiphrah's eyes flew to Chanoch. 'Has Chanoch told you about my request?'

'He has. Is it still what you want, after this?'

'I'll need time to think about it, but… Jared sought me out, Abba. He was crazy, but between the pushing and scrambling, he said he couldn't believe Chanoch had refused Talia and chosen me. That I must have some secret attraction. That I must—' she stopped and flushpol;;;;ed a deep pink. 'That I must have given myself to Chanoch – I haven't, Abba. I promise I haven't!'

'I believe you,' Set said, also looking Chanoch's way.

'He said if I behaved that way, I should give him some too. Oh, it was horrible. He had waited for you to be back in the valley, Chanoch. When he saw you there, he knew I would be alone, so he came here, especially to—'

Now Shiphrah broke, all merriment gone as the memories flooded back. Tears streamed down her face and she heaved in irregular bursts. Set gathered her into his arms and rocked her from side to side as if she were a little child.

'I don't think I can face them again, Abba. What if everyone thinks the same way as he does? What if...'

'Shhh, shhh. No, my love, no. No-one else thinks that way.'

'But I can understand it. It doesn't make any sense that he chose me.'

Chanoch felt like the outsider in the room as Shiphrah continued to cry in her father's arms. How could she feel those things? How could she value herself so little? What Jared had said was poison, poison from the deceiving viper himself. He stood and backed away.

'Chanoch.' Shiphrah held out an arm to him and beckoned. 'Do you despise me now?'

'No!' It was enough to propel him back to her side. 'A thousand times, no.'

'You don't think me sullied?'

'Of course not. Besides, you said Jared didn't succeed.'

'He didn't.'

'Oh Shiphrah, even if he had— Your bravery, your attitude to it all… I love you more than ever.'

'Then marry me,' she replied. 'Marry me and take me away from here. Take me to the land of wandering.'

New Beginnings

Two weeks later, word came that Enosh, Adam and another had apprehended Jared. They'd tracked his footprints all the way to the Euphrates, where he'd been trying, unsuccessfully, to find a river crossing. He was brought back to the valley and detained with a guard while Adam tried to figure out what to do with him.

Set hadn't gone down to the valley, but stayed with Yemima, following Ima's advice. The strain on his face was evident to all – he looked like he'd aged a century – but he'd remained calm for Shiphrah's sake. Set's wife came up the day after Enosh went down. She cared for Shiphrah as only a mother can and wept with the knowledge her daughter would soon be leaving. But they all agreed to it, even Ima. None wanted to put Shiphrah through further humiliation.

'Are you sure you still care for me?' Shiphrah asked Chanoch after they heard the news about Jared. 'Nobody would blame you for backing out.'

Chanoch slipped his hand into hers. He was nervous about embracing her again. He didn't want to cause her pain by association, even though her body had healed.

On the other hand, perhaps his nerves were contributing to hers. Did she need reassurance?

'My feelings for you haven't changed at all. I'm just unsure whether…'

'What?'

He decided that honesty was the best course. 'Do you want me to hold you as I did before? For I want nothing more than to take you in my arms, but I don't want you to be scared.'

Shiphrah released a long breath. 'That's what you've been worried about? Chanoch, I'm not frightened of you. Quite the opposite. You make me feel safe; I want you to hold me forever.' She pulled her hand from his and threaded her arm around his back.

'Are you sure?' he asked, leaning his head onto hers as she snuggled into his shoulder.

'I'm sure.'

They married the following week. Adam came up to the hills to take the ceremony, along with Chavah, Shiphrah's immediate family, and other selected individuals. Shiphrah didn't want everyone there, and no-one suggested it.

That first night, they slept in a cave in the woods, for no spare hut was available, and Chanoch was used to caves anyway.

'You'll have to get used to them too,' he said, as he kissed his wife. 'We haven't built any huts in Nod, and we certainly won't make any on the journey.'

Shiphrah kissed him back, and he revelled in their closeness, away from any prying eyes. 'I don't mind where I sleep as long as I'm with you.'

'We shall have to put up with Ima's company for the first little while, I'm afraid.'

'Then let's make the most of the time we have alone before we leave.'

And they did.

Chanoch hitched a large pack of supplies onto his back and slung two water-skins over his shoulders. Carrying for two was considerably heavier than what he'd borne on his journey to the land between the rivers just a season before. Now almond blossom scented the breeze and pulling flax consumed the workers' days. Soon they would be harvesting barley, and Chanoch wondered if they would make it home before his abba journeyed to the coastlands to glean from the wild grains there.

'Ready Ima?' he asked as she too lifted a water-skin to her shoulders. Yemima had filled their packs with bread, fruit and wool blankets, and the only thing Shiphrah carried was a sheepskin to aid her comfort at night.

'Ready.'

After an emotional goodbye with their relatives, they walked down the hill, journeying the opposite way they'd come, for Ima had taken heed of Adam's words about Shimon. At another crossing place much further downstream on the Tigris, one of their cousins had a raft, and had offered to see them across. Adam informed them it was where Havel and Awan crossed many years ago on the way back from finding medicine for Kayin – a wider, shallower and calmer spot.

The crossing was unusual. None of them had been on a raft before, and they went one at a time to reduce the wobble. Once safely across, Chanoch considered the peaks ahead and to their left. The mountain pass would be trickier from this direction, Ima had said, for there was no hill country to break up the first part of it. But there was no rush. It was more important to be safe.

For the few days, they journeyed in the mornings, rested in the heat of the day and then continued a short way further before nightfall. It was as much as Shiphrah could cope with, and by the sixth day, she was exhausted and in agony.

'Lets take a day of rest,' Ima said. 'Two if we need it.'

They'd found a spot near a tributary of the Tigris, where the water was fresh. Ima was confident she knew roughly where she was, but Chanoch felt less so. What if they got lost in the mountains? They might walk for days getting nowhere, and what would that do for Shiphrah's health? At least there was plenty of food available – even if it largely consisted of roots they must boil, mushrooms and edible flowers. It was too early for summer fruit, but Ima was used to gleaning from the land and excellent at finding food in the most obscure places.

They built up a shelter and, as Shiphrah rested, Chanoch collected wood for the fire and Ima prepared some ingredients for a light soup. By nightfall, Shiphrah was feeling much better and joined them by the fire. Chanoch wrapped his arms and a blanket around her as they sipped more soup. With the fire guarding them against predators, they sang several songs – still quietly, for they were always careful not to draw attention to themselves, just in case.

After a little while, stillness descended. Chanoch was just about to ask Shiphrah how she felt about continuing the following day, when Ima placed a finger to her lips.

What was it? Had she heard something?

Then she smiled. 'Welcome, Yael. Do join us.'

A faint gasp came from behind.

Chanoch spun his head to see a knife at Ima's throat.

Ima didn't flinch. 'You must be hungry. Come and eat.'

A flash of blonde – golden in the firelight – accompanied the crunching of twigs and leaves as Yael stepped out from between the branches, knife still poised. 'I'm here to capture you, not to eat.'

Chanoch's body tensed. He wanted to grab Yael, to wrestle the knife from her grasp, but there was no way he could do it in time. Ima would surely get sliced. Yet Ima was entirely calm. How?

'I don't see why you can't do both.' Ima chuckled. 'I know you've been following us for a day or so. If you wanted to attack us, you would have done so already.'

Yael snorted.

'I won't resist you, Yael. Let me pour you some soup.'

The young woman sniffed, then allowed her knife to retreat just far enough for Ima to move, while remaining close enough to strike. Ima poured soup into her empty bowl and held it out. 'Come sit.'

'How did you know?' Chanoch asked as Yael tentatively crouched next to Ima. 'I hadn't noticed her.'

Ima chuckled again. 'You are a newly wed with its associated distractions. I am still constantly aware.'

Chanoch scratched his arm, struggling to believe he'd missed the signs, for he was used to a fugitive's life too, and had been taught the skills since childhood. Shiphrah really must be distracting him.

'So, you found a wife then.' Yael scowled at him and spoke between gulps of soup, holding the bowl with one hand while her other still held the knife. 'Is she the only woman who'd have you?'

Chanoch bristled, but before he could defend her, Shiphrah spoke. 'Actually, the most beautiful woman in the valley was interested in my husband, but he chose me.'

As Shiphrah kissed Chanoch on the cheek, Yael rolled her eyes. 'I knew you were strange.'

Chanoch should have been offended, but despite knowing her for so little time, he felt that nothing Yael did could offend or surprise him. Well, except holding a knife to Ima's throat after following them for two days.

'So, I take it that Shimon sent you after us?' Ima said, removing Yael's empty bowl from her hand and refilling it.

This darkened the young woman's countenance further. 'He arrived home about a week ago,' she said. 'When he found out you were in the valley, he sent us all out – my brothers and me – to guard one path across the mountains each. He didn't dare cross the river.'

'So, why didn't you capture us earlier?' Ima asked.

Yael slurped noisily. 'Clearly, you already knew I was here.'

'That's not it. You must have seen us long before I sensed you. Something held you back, Yael.'

After shoving her empty bowl back at Ima, Yael crossed her arms, saying nothing. Finally the knife was out of sight, but Chanoch knew she could retrieve it as fast as lightning.

'Why not take me back to your father?' Ima pressed. 'Perhaps you couldn't capture three of us, but you could take one. You're a hunter. You could have picked me off from the group, or told your brothers where we were. Yet, you have followed silently.'

Chanoch also didn't understand. 'Ima, if you knew Yael was there, why didn't you call her out before?'

At this, Ima smiled. 'Because I usually find that songs of praise are the most effective shield against danger. Am I right, Yael?'

Yael's top lip curled, like she was going to bare her teeth. Then she abruptly broke, sinking her face into her hands and sobbing. The knife fell to her feet. Looking entirely unsurprised, Ima shuffled closer to her, put an arm around her shoulders and pulled her into a hug.

'Abba beat Ima,' Yael cried. 'I've seen him do it before, but not like this. She was bruised all over. He said she was lucky he didn't kill her for letting you go… I was so angry! I knew which path you'd take – I knew about the raft. I volunteered to take the path furthest south because I wanted to find you and punish you for what happened to Ima. It was your fault Abba was so angry! Then I saw you, and I… I couldn't immediately do it. You…' she pointed at Chanoch. 'I thought you so, so foolish, but you were the only person who ever showed me kindness, for no apparent reason, and there you were with your wife, holding her up as she struggled and stumbled.'

It seemed for all her bluster, Yael did have a sensitive side…

'I worked myself up to it overnight. I was going to capture you early this morning. Then, I heard you sing...'

Stroking Yael's hair, Ima encouraged her to continue.

'You sang of Yahweh being your light and your salvation. At first I thought, what salvation? Yahweh can't save them from me. Then you sang, *Whom shall I fear?* And I realised – I want what you have. I don't want to live in fear of Abba anymore, nor to live in the darkness. I don't want my ima's life.'

Chanoch looked into Shiphrah's face – how was she taking this? He wanted to believe Yael, but this might still be a ruse. What if Shimon came out of hiding with his sons and took them all captive? Shiphrah betrayed no such suspicion. Her earnest expression showed only compassion for the younger woman.

'Then come with us, Yael,' Shiphrah said.

Yael looked up and stared at them. 'You don't even know me. I just insulted you!'

'It's nothing I haven't heard before. Come with us to Nod.'

'No.' Yael shook her head. 'Abba would kill me. I must return, taking Awan.'

'If Shimon can't find Kayin then he won't find you,' Shiphrah replied. 'Living with Kayin and Awan in Nod is the safest place you could be. Moreover, they can teach you about Yahweh.'

Yael's wet eyes shone in the firelight, brighter than her hair. 'Truly? You would have me?'

'It would be our pleasure,' Ima confirmed.

Having Yael with them proved to be exceedingly helpful. She knew the terrain intimately and several times, when Ima suggested a particular route, Yael pointed them to a better one. At first, Chanoch was nervous, thinking she might be leading them into a trap or back towards one of Shimon's outposts, but after a week or so with no sign of trickery, he relaxed and took her at her word.

Ima showed no such fear, and nor had Shiphrah. Both seemed to accept Yael's story on face value, and the more time they spent together, the closer the three women became. Chanoch wondered if Yahweh might have a plan for Yael beyond keeping them safe on their journey. Might she suit one of his younger brothers in time?

The heat of early summer was clinging to his skin when Chanoch at last saw the Great Lake in the distance, from halfway down the final mountain. He sighed in contentment. *Home.* Two people had left that winter, and now four returned. Four more wanderers entering the land of Nod.

'It's rather barren, isn't it?' Shiphrah said, surveying the plain they must cross to reach the lake.

'It's not all like this.' He wrapped his arms around her. 'The crossing to the lake is harsh, but after that, there's plenty of greenery. And at least there are no more mountains to climb. We'll soon be home.' *Back to Abba.*

Yael appeared, chewing on a rodent that she'd caught and roasted. 'I'm looking forward to meeting the man I've been hunting my entire life.'

Chanoch's back stiffened until she shoved him with her free arm. 'I'm not going to do anything. Besides, my father said he's huge!'

Chanoch glanced at Ima. She was smiling and bore the same look she'd had on her way to see her family. This time, the longing was for her husband. Chanoch understood now. For he had found the impossible – a woman he loved as much as Ima loved Abba. A woman who loved him enough to leave the land between the rivers.

AUTHOR'S NOTE

Those who follow my writing will know that I love an appendix. I wasn't intending to write one for this little novella, but for the sake of those who might read this before anything else, I thought I would just include this little note on names.

Chanoch is the Hebrew name for Enoch, the son of Cain. Of course, I use the spelling Kayin for Cain, and I hope you realised who I meant – for Chanoch's father is the Cain of Cain and Abel fame. This Enoch is not to be confused with the later one, who 'walked with the Lord and then was no more, because God took him away.' That Enoch is a descendent of Seth.

Seth is a name I render as Set. This is because there is no 'th' sound in Hebrew. It should actually be Sheyt but this doesn't sound good in English, so I used Set, similar to the Egyptian, Seti.

Awan, Chanoch's mother, has a name borrowed from the book of Jubilees. There is no hard 'J' sound in Hebrew, so Jemima becomes Yemima and Jael becomes Yael. I left the name Enosh as is, because despite the similarity to Enoch in English, the name Enosh in Hebrew is roughly similar. Enosh means 'mortal man' and we see Enosh is a less spiritual character than his father, Set.

Chavah is Eve, and another example of where the Hebrew differs significantly from the English. The pronunciation of this first sound 'Ch' at the beginning of Chavah, Chanoch, Channah and Chayim is a guttural H sound, not 'ch' as in cheese. As you can see, it's a common sound!

If you enjoyed the story, and want to know more about the other characters, you can read about them in:

The Wanderer Scorned
Kayin's Story

The Wanderer Reborn
Awan's story

The Wanderer's Sister
Avigail's story

The Wanderer's Legacy
Adah's story

Chanoch is an important part of Adah's story and also has a cameo role in *The Wanderer Scorned*, and *The Wanderer Reborn*. More about them over the page.

N.W.

THE WANDERER SCORNED

Book 1 in *The Wanderer* Series

By NATASHA WOODCRAFT

Sin is crouching at the door, ready to pounce. You must master it before it masters you.

Kayin is The Wanderer: a legend shrouded in a curse. A man untouchable, unable to farm or settle.

Centuries after the horrendous act that defines his life, Kayin recounts his soul-stirring chronicle, exposing the far-reaching fallout of his parents' expulsion from Eden and revisiting the moments that shattered his youthful faith. Then came forbidden love and rejection, driving a wedge irrevocably between Kayin and his brother, with tragic consequences.

Why did God scorn Kayin's sacrifice? What transpired during that final, fateful encounter in the field?

ISBN: 978-1-915034-82-3

Ebook: https://books2read.com/u/3GzjAK

THE WANDERER REBORN

Book 2 in *The Wanderer* Series

By NATASHA WOODCRAFT

Can hope triumph after the first murder?

Awan is reeling in agony. The man she loved has murdered her twin brother then disappeared. Tormented by his actions, recovery seems an impossible dream. When her well-meaning father tries to marry her to someone else, Awan refuses, knowing her heart is broken beyond repair.

Questioning the God who claims to stand for justice, Awan struggles to forgive. How can she when the murderer is still out there? Then she makes a terrible mistake that threatens to fracture her family further. In obedience to God's call, she sets out on a perilous pilgrimage, not knowing if the end will mean redemption or death.

ISBN: 978-1-915034-84-7

Ebook: https://books2read.com/u/4Dn0yA

THE WANDERER'S LEGACY

Book 3 in *The Wanderer* series

by NATASHA WOODCRAFT

Adah lives trapped between the life she longed for and the life she chose. Barren and desperate, she has failed to produce an heir for her once devoted husband, Lamech. As Lamech becomes increasingly unpredictable and domineering, Adah is drawn to legends about the mysterious Wanderer.

When Lamech takes a second wife, Adah's world shatters – sending her fleeing to her family home. Here, a fragile sense of freedom awakens long-buried hopes. But a secret grows within her – a secret that will propel her back into the heart of danger.

With survival a daily struggle, can a legend offer Adah salvation? Or does someone else hold the power to help her dwell in safety?

ISBN: 978-1-915034-88-5

Ebook: https://books2read.com/wandererslegacy

ABOUT THE AUTHOR

Natasha Woodcraft lives in a slightly crumbling farmhouse in Lincolnshire, UK, with her husband, four sons and a menagerie of animals.

Though she has a first-class honours degree in theology, Natasha's first love is stories, which she believes have power to communicate deep truth and transform lives. Her published novels explore God's redemptive purposes for messy people living in biblical times.

Also a songwriter, Natasha peppers her emotional prose with poetry and song. She's a founder member of the *Kingdom Story Writers* and a director at Broad Place Publishing.

ALSO FROM THE PUBLISHER

They Whisper About Us
By Joy Vee

A tea tin. Owned by one girl, found by another over half a century later.
What mysteries does it hide?

Vera dreams of rising thorough the Kirov Ballet and maybe becoming a People's Artist. Fay is a pastor's kid, disillusioned with her parents' faith, who attends a theatre summer programme in the hope of improving her skills. The girls' plans do not work out as they'd hoped, and their lives become entwined when Fay accidentally finds an old tea tin.

An intriguing split time-line story, alternating between Leningrad in 1960's and modern day England.